For a long moment
they stood motionless,

locked in each other's arms. Then, without warning, something nudged Bric. At first he thought Kara was pushing him away. But her head still rested under his chin, and her slender arms were still locked around his waist. When he felt the jostle again, a definite thump against his midsection, he squeezed his eyes shut, overpowered by an unexpected sensation.

Kara leaned back. "Sorry," she murmured, flushing. "I don't know what came over me. Dizzy, I guess."

"Don't apologize. I liked holding you." His voice was rough with feeling. "And the baby."

Dear Reader,

Among the stellar authors in our January lineup is Lynda Trent, well-known for her weighty historical novels. What keeps her coming back to Silhouette **Special Edition**? Here's how she explains it:

"I write for Silhouette Special Edition to share a romantic fantasy with my readers, an emotional adventure in which a woman might be an heiress, a commoner or a Mata Hari . . . and still be loved by the perfect man. Within the broad scope of a Special Edition, she might dare to love a dangerous man; she might chance everything for a noble cause. I want to weave a tapestry of romance blossoming, of dreams fulfilled, and I want to share it with other dreamers."

Like the piratical hero of Lynda Trent's *Like Strangers*, the authors and editors of Silhouette **Special Edition** want to knock on the door to your heart . . . and open it to all the possibilities life and love have to offer.

Share your tastes and preferences with us. Each and every month we strive to offer you something new, something *special*. Let us know how we're doing!

Happy new year,

Leslie Kazanjian, Senior Editor
Silhouette Books
300 East 42nd Street
New York, N.Y. 10017

MADELYN DOHRN
Labor of Love

Silhouette Special Edition

Published by Silhouette Books New York

America's Publisher of Contemporary Romance

This book is dedicated with love
To Jim—the brick in my life
and
To Clyde—whose teaching is love

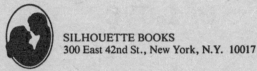

SILHOUETTE BOOKS
300 East 42nd St., New York, N.Y. 10017

ISBN: 0-373-09501-5

First Silhouette Books printing January 1989

MADELYN DOHRN

lives in a small Ohio town with her professor husband and family. After years of teaching college English, she one day decided to try her hand at writing a romance and soon found herself captivated by the task. When she's not in front of her word processor, she likes to travel, read, entertain friends and keep fit with dancerobics.

Underlined places are fictitious.

Chapter One

The chalk slipped from between Kara Reynolds's fingers and shattered on the hardwood floor. As she slowly stooped to collect the fragments, she spied Sam Linskey reaching across his desk to close his hand over Delia McCann's palm.

"Have you finished your essay yet, Sam?" Kara called out.

The musical vibrancy in his teacher's voice brought the high school senior up short. "Uh, not quite, Mrs. Reynolds." He snatched up his pen, then made it fairly fly across the almost empty sheet of paper before him.

Kara smiled at the young man. She knew he was more than a little embarrassed at having been caught holding Delia's hand. Something akin to jealousy but more like regret clutched at Kara's heart.

As she wended her way from the blackboard to the last row of desks, her thoughts trailed back in time to the summer she'd been about Delia's age. The summer she'd turned eighteen and met Edmund Reynolds. He was three years older than she. Tall, lean and strikingly handsome. She would never forget how a soft gasp had lodged in her throat at her first glimpse of his finely sculpted features, which were set off to perfection by wavy blond hair and brilliant blue eyes.

Kara pensively ran a palm across her stomach. All the while they'd gone together, Edmund had maintained a gentlemanly restraint that had at first flattered, then frustrated her. In time she'd longed for more than chaste kisses and tepid embraces. But any fumbling attempts on her part to take their relationship further had invariably ended in disappointment.

Over and over Kara had had to remind herself that she was fortunate to have a man who treated her like a lady, one who believed in curbing passion until after marriage. Too late she realized that Edmund wasn't really interested in her, that his reserve was nothing more than an excuse. Yet, lovesick fool that she was, she'd yearned for him to look at her the way Sam so often eyed Delia.

Kara caught her lower lip between her teeth and ruthlessly kept her mind in the present. Little Joey Engel had his hand up. She moved toward him across the well-oiled planks of the one-room schoolhouse.

Poor Joey. He looked about as unhappy, bewildered and lost as she had six months earlier.

"What can I help you with?" Kara asked as she awkwardly squeezed into a vacant seat. When the six-year-old turned sad gray eyes on her, she yielded to the impulse and gave his bony shoulder a reassuring squeeze.

"I don't understand what to do here." Joey peered down at the arithmetic book in front of him and pointed to an addition problem.

"I can see why that's giving you trouble," Kara confided. "Maybe this will help you understand." She reached into the pocket of her loosely flowing russet jumper, pulled out ten brand-new pennies and lined them up at the top of Joey's desk. "What I want you to do is divide these pennies according to the numbers given in the problem. You've learned how to count to ten, so you should be able to do that. Right?"

Joey nodded, then proceeded to sort the pennies into three separate stacks.

"Count your pennies one by one, and tell me how many you have in all," she said.

"Ten."

"Now we know that five plus three plus two equals ten. Can you see how we get that answer?"

Joey stared at the money, then shook his head.

"It's quite simple. We take the first two numbers and add them together. Five plus three. You've added two numbers together. What's the answer?"

"Eight."

"Okay, now add your eight to two, and what do you get?"

"Ten!" Joey's freckled face lit up and he gave Kara a broad grin, revealing a gap where two front teeth were missing.

"I think you should be able to do the rest of the problems on the page. Remember, all you have to do is add the first two numbers together, then add that answer to the third number. Understand now?"

"Sure, teacher. You always make everything easy."

Kara's smile was half indulgent, half scolding. "Doesn't this teacher have a name, Joey?" she gently prodded him.

"Mrs. Reynolds." His shoulders sagged at the verbal slip.

"Thank you for remembering." Kara brushed an unruly shock of hair off Joey's forehead. "I think you deserve a reward for catching on so quickly to the problems. Why don't you keep these to work with?"

Joey looked up, his eyes as bright as the pennies Kara offered. "Gee, thanks!"

After painstakingly pushing herself to her feet, Kara braced a palm against the small of her back and leaned first to one side and then the other in an attempt to relieve a slight ache in her lower spine.

Back at her desk, she continued to think about Joey. With seven years of teaching experience, she didn't need a set of standardized test scores to prove he was an intelligent child. But the little boy had been so incredibly deprived that he had yet to be taught a lot of things most six-year-olds already knew. Still, he was quick. Usually she had to explain something only once before he grasped it.

Kara had been on Perry's Island but a few days when Delia's mother had filled her in on Joey's background. It had been a hot, humid day in late August, and they'd been relaxing on the McCann front porch, sipping lemonade. In the flattened speech typical of the islanders, Mrs. McCann, a stocky, affable woman, had recounted how Phyllis Engel had run off with a bass player in a jazz band, abandoning her husband and two-year-old son. Which had come as a surprise to no one except Joey's father. After all, Phyllis was an outsider, a mainlander, and they never lasted long on the islands. Only those born and bred to the place were hardy enough to endure the bitterly cold Lake Erie winters, the exhausting work of the vineyards and, worst of all, the sense of isolation.

As she'd watched the older woman's green wicker rocker creak back and forth, Kara had wondered if Mrs. McCann was trying to warn her in some way. It had even crossed her mind that the woman judged her too weak in body or spirit to withstand the rigors of Perry's Island, to face the demands of a rather antiquated one-room schoolhouse, to keep track of children working on several different grade levels. But Kara hadn't had a chance to ponder the possibilities—or to take offense—because her hostess had barely paused to catch her breath before launching into the details surrounding the death of Tom Engel.

Mrs. McCann had rambled on, her speech colored by the local idiom. Seemed as if he'd taken to drink after his wife skipped off. Did only enough work to keep him in whiskey. Pretty much shut out the boy. If it hadn't been for some of the island women, the little tyke'd never've made it.

Then early that summer—just a few weeks before Kara's arrival—Tom had taken his boat out to do some fishing. Drunk as a skunk, he was, Mrs. McCann had intoned. Nothing new in that. Nothing new in his goin' fishing, either. But he didn't come home that night. Three days later his body washed up a few miles east of Sandusky. Nobody knew for sure. They supposed his boat had capsized and Tom had drowned in a drunken stupor.

Kara remembered suppressing a slight shiver despite the blazing heat of the late-summer day. When she'd asked if Joey's lot had improved with the death of his father, she'd learned that in one respect it had. Joey was now living with Edith Parker, Tom's older sister, and her husband. The Parkers had already raised seven children, but they were God-fearing people, determined to do their duty by the little boy. Too bad they didn't appear to have a whole lot of love left over for their young nephew, Mrs. McCann had said.

"Mrs. Reynolds, it's about time for us to leave."

Sam's voice sliced into her thoughts. "Good heavens, it can't be eleven-thirty already." Kara glanced at the massive clock that for nearly a century had announced to fidgety schoolchildren how much longer they had to squirm in their seats. Then she nodded at Delia and Sam. "I'll see you two in the morning. And, Sam, don't forget that paper you were supposed to turn in fifteen minutes ago."

Sheepishly, he looked past his teacher. "I'll have it finished. Don't worry. And it'll be a good one. The best I've ever written."

"I'm counting on it, Sam." Kara knew his essay wouldn't have to show much improvement to be, as he promised, the best he'd ever done. Sam wasn't exactly *into* writing, but then she couldn't really blame him. The Linskeys had run the winery on Perry's Island for nearly a hundred years—and this last generation did things pretty much the same way as the first. Tall, sturdy, already looking more man than boy, Sam would take over from his father just as Wayne Linskey had taken over from his. A ready-made job provided scant motivation for learning how to write a theme, even though the county board's senior English curriculum called for Sam's mastery of the technique. After their May graduation, he and Delia would undoubtedly settle down together and raise a family. Kara didn't exactly approve of anyone that young marrying. Yet after the mess she'd made of her own life, who was she to say what others should do with theirs?

A restless stirring not unlike the rapid flutter of a hummingbird's wings coursed through Kara's middle. She hugged her arms around her stomach and focused her attention on the remaining students. It would be three and a half hours before another school day was over. More than enough time, she concluded, for Joey's reading and writing, Ruth and Ralph Conlen's fourth-grade history and math, and Billy Oldt's sixth-grade spelling and geography.

But for now Ralph was beside her, plucking at her sleeve.

John Brickner stood behind the double doors separating entryway from classroom. He stepped aside as Delia and Sam brushed past him, quizzical expressions furrowing their brows. No sooner had they snatched up heavy wool coats and bolted outside into a brisk winter wind than he'd again opened one of the doors a crack and peered into the large room. His gaze traveled from desks so old they still boasted inkwells, to a battered upright piano engraved with the initials of former students, to a huge globe supported on a claw-footed brass stand. A large wood-burning stove, obviously the sole source of heat, stood in front of the first row of desks. All this antiquity was in startling contrast to the late-model computer situated on a corner table.

What really riveted Bric's interest, though, and what had kept him from barging in when he'd arrived five minutes earlier was the woman seated at her desk near the blackboard. Ordinarily he wouldn't have hesitated to interrupt, but he'd hated to disturb that look of soft contemplation as she listened intently to the boy at her side. And now that she was patiently explaining a math problem to the youngster, he found himself not wanting to cut short the music of that whispery voice, so calm, so serene it fairly waltzed over his senses.

He suspected it would only be a few minutes more until they broke for lunch. So he waited. Listening, watching.

The boy, Bric noticed, hung on to the woman's every word, staring up at her almost as if he were looking into the face of an angel. He couldn't blame the kid for falling under her spell. She was a vision, all right. Sunlight streaming through the window glinted off golden strands that were threaded through her auburn hair. Almost like a halo, he marveled, and a fitting frame for what he deemed the most flawless face he'd ever laid eyes on. The woman's high sweeping forehead, straight delicate nose and long slender neck gave her an undisputed air of elegance and grace. As if that weren't enough, she had the kind of petal-smooth skin that invited a man to reach out and run a finger over its satiny perfection.

Bric waited for perhaps another minute before the lunch break was announced. He felt the door directly in front of him being pushed from the opposite side. When it barely budged, he grabbed the handle and gave a firm tug. Years of moisture-laden lake air had warped the wood into a misshapen slab that stubbornly refused to give way except under the most forceful pressure. Looking down, he saw a half-moon scraped tellingly into the floor. Inconvenient was the first word that came to mind. Dangerous, the second.

A small child stumbled through the door, which had been alternately jerked and shoved open. "Who are you?"

Smiling down into the inquisitive face of the boy, who couldn't be more than five or six, he joked off-handedly, "The delivery man."

"What're you delivering?"

He pointed to a heavy carton stamped with the manufacturer's name: Warren Brothers Educational Supply Company.

"Ah, the bookcase I've been waiting for."

Bric turned to stare into the most fascinating eyes he'd ever seen. Large and wide set, they weren't a clear blue, but a rarer shade. Lighter, smokier. They reminded him of lilacs right before they burst into bloom. Violet, that's what they were, he decided. An arresting complement to the rich mane of reddish-brown hair. Up close, she was even more breath snatching than at a distance.

As she stepped from behind the large carton, Bric's gaze drifted lower and came to rest on the swollen mound of her stomach. Pregnant. My God! She's pregnant! Feeling vaguely as if he'd been struck broadside with a ton of bricks, he stood stock-still as Kara heedlessly edged her way past him and grabbed hold of the carton.

While he struggled to regain a semblance of equilibrium, a wave of self-disgust washed over him. Not two minutes before, he'd practically entertained erotic fantasies about a mother-to-be!

Before his mind fully registered what she was doing, Kara had begun to half push, half drag the carton toward the still open door. Immediately Bric came to. "Hold on a minute." In a single stride he was beside her. "I'm the one being paid to deliver this thing."

In her haste Kara had given the newcomer only a cursory glance before tackling the carton. If she'd had any intention of arguing with the firm grip on her shoulder, it faded when she swiveled and met with the man's face. It was handsome in a rawboned sort of way, compelling in spite of the clenched jaws, which hardened his well-molded lips, or even the scowl that cut deep lines into his brow. Dimly Kara wondered if she was in some way responsible for the man's show of irritation. At the same time she considered what it would take to loosen up that mouth and make it smile.

"Then be my guest, Mr. . . . ." Kara eyed him questioningly.

"Brickner," he supplied. "John Brickner. Most people make it Bric." He lifted the large carton as if it were no heavier than a box of crackers and elbowed his way through the door.

Eyeing his hard, masculine contours, which were evident even under the fleece-lined flight jacket and faded jeans, she remarked, "It suits you."

Bric was somewhat taken aback. Now, what did she mean by that? If he didn't know better, he'd swear she was flirting. But pregnant women didn't flirt. Or did they? Try as he might, he didn't have the power to stem the ripple of awareness she'd sent sluicing through him. Damn! He ought to be horsewhipped for reacting to an expectant mother that way.

But maybe he wasn't entirely to blame. Maybe his ready response was only nature's ironic protest of the trick life had played on him.

"I'd better get on with it," Bric growled.

Kara saw that the scowl was back on his face, darker than ever.

"They'll be wondering what happened to me if I take too long." He searched the pockets of his jacket.

"They?"

"The men at the winery. I'm picking up some equipment to be repaired."

Kara tilted her head and studied him. "Oh, you fix machinery?"

"Nope. Just a fly-boy." Bric unzipped his jacket and dug a hand into his right jeans pocket.

"You work for the local airline, then."

"Mmm." The sound neither confirmed nor denied her assumption.

"I heard Ben Jackson decided to sell Erie Islands Air Service. You like the new owner?"

"Mmm," Bric repeated, purposely fixing his attention on a thorough search of his pockets. He was determined to keep the small talk to a minimum and get out of there as fast as possible. The woman had him so discombobulated he could barely put two intelligent words together.

"Are you usually this communicative?" Kara asked, openly amused.

Bric's probing hand stilled in his pocket. "What did you say?"

"I was wondering what you thought of your new boss."

"My new boss?" His brow wrinkled as he considered her question. "I don't have one, unless you count my partner. You're looking at half of the new corporation."

It was Kara's turn to fall back on an "Mmm." He certainly didn't look like the business type to her.

"Say, do you have something I could use to pry out these staples? I don't seem to have my pocketknife on me."

"Of course." Kara moved in the direction of her small apartment, which was attached to the side of the schoolhouse. The children were sitting around her table, demolishing the remains of sack lunches they'd earlier claimed from storage shelves in the cool entryway. Kara quickly found what she was looking for and, when she returned, placed the shoe box in Bric's large hands. He took off the lid and stared at a hammer, three screwdrivers and a pair of pliers. "This the extent of your tools?"

"I'm afraid so."

Bric pictured his own fully equipped workroom and smiled at the contrast. "This should do it," he said as he retrieved the lone hammer.

Kara watched silently as Bric pried thick industrial staples from the carton. Without a doubt he was a vibrantly masculine man, a shade rough around the edges. The fine lines etching his dark brown eyes and the hint of gray in his thick black hair only added to his attractiveness.

She'd meant it when she'd said his name suited him. The directness of his gaze reflected obstinacy, as well as strength and character. She wondered if he was always so sparing with words. In spite of his reticence—or perhaps because of it—he gave the impression of solid dependability. Of being a man a woman could count on.

That thought had Kara suddenly stiffening her spine and lifting her chin. If there was anything Edmund had taught her, she reminded herself bitterly, it was to depend on no one.

With the jogging of her memory came the need for her to put some distance between them. Walking over to the piano and slowly lowering herself onto the bench, Kara willed herself to look at anything except the man opening the sturdy packing box. He'd tossed aside his flight jacket, giving her an unimpeded view of sleek muscles alternately rippling and bunching beneath his work shirt. Self-consciously she fidgeted with the folds of her jumper, arranging their fullness over the swell of her abdomen.

After pulling wooden parts and hardware from the shipping case, Bric remarked dryly, "Lucky for you, all you need is a screwdriver to put the thing together. Think you can handle it from here?''

''I'll manage.'' Kara levered herself up from the bench and came toward Bric. ''I've held you up long enough. Thanks for breaking into this for me. It would have taken me forever.''

''More than happy to be of service.'' Automatically Bric extended a hand. ''It was nice meeting you, uh . . .'' He smiled. ''You never told me your name.''

''Kara. Kara Reynolds.'' She held out her arm in return and impulsively laid her left palm on top of their joined hands.

He knew it was a simple gesture of appreciation, but the softness of her touch exerted an indefinable pull on him. Not exactly a flare of passion but something equally primitive, as fully profound. Staring down at her hand, Bric discovered her unadorned ring finger. No gold band. He lifted a puzzled brow, his expression immobile. ''Nice to meet you . . . Ms. Reynolds.''

Kara's eyes followed the line of his vision, and she guessed at the conclusion he'd drawn. She slid her left hand from atop his and distractedly combed through her hair. For reasons she couldn't name, she wanted him to know that she had been married, that her baby was legitimate. ''Mrs.,'' she corrected, her voice holding a faint reproof.

The slight amendment curved Bric's lips into a lopsided smile. Strange, until that very second he hadn't considered the man in her life. Stupid of him. He should have known the absence of a wedding band proved nothing. After all, hadn't his sisters removed their rings when pregnancy had swelled their fingers?

Kara looked up into warm brown eyes. "But I...my husband...that is, I lost my husband..." Her voice faltered as pride stemmed the flow of words. She couldn't possibly admit to a total stranger that she hadn't been able to hang on to Edmund, that he'd preferred another woman to her.

Bric drew in a sharp breath, suddenly flooded by an odd mix of emotions. Instinctively he tightened his grip and resisted an urge to draw her into his arms. Purely in sympathy? He couldn't say. He knew only that it was time to leave, that he should let go of her hand. But he was reluctant to break contact with the warm flesh pressed against his callused fingers. Without his realizing it, the rough pad of his thumb stroked the sensitive flesh along the base of her index finger.

The rhythmic touch stirred something deep within Kara. This time, though, the movement had nothing to do with the baby growing in her womb.

Chapter Two

Teacher!"

Kara looked up from where she was helping Ruth with a division problem and fixed her first grader with an admonishing frown. "Joey, you make me feel like a generic person. Someone without a real name."

The boy's head dropped as his lower lip came out in an apologetic pout. "I'm sorry, Mrs. Reynolds. I keep forgetting."

Kara smiled. It was impossible for her to be provoked with Joey for more than an instant. He was the kind of forlorn child who immediately wormed his way into one's heart, made a comfortable place for himself and curled up for the duration. As a teacher, she couldn't show favoritism. But some children naturally appealed to her more than others. Joey was one of them.

"If you can wait a second, I'll be right over. I want to check Ruth's answer first."

"It ain't me wants you. It's him again." Joey thumbed over his shoulder to a tall figure standing just inside the door.

As her glance swung to the back of the room, Kara drew in a quick breath. So intent had she been on explaining long division to Ruth that she hadn't heard anyone come in. Even before the intruder stepped from the shadowed entryway, she had identified his rangy frame. "Mr. Brickner," she acknowledged, her voice laced with surprise.

"Sorry to interrupt, but I was on the island. Delivering those repairs to the winery." An unnatural silence reigned while four childish faces eyed him with undisguised curiosity. Bric felt as awkward as a blundering adolescent vying for the attention of the prettiest girl in class. "I guess," he stammered, half turning around, "the equipment reminded me...your door. I noticed the other day it sticks. I thought you might like it fixed."

And that's the *only* reason he'd come back, Bric told himself as his gaze lingered on the softly feminine woman before him. She was more beautiful than he remembered. He watched, mesmerized, as a faint flush crept into her cheeks. Was it his imagination, or had her breathing really quickened?

Berating himself for the direction his thoughts were taking, he rushed on. "I know this isn't a good time, but I thought if you're going to be here after school, I could plane that door down for you. It's got to be a nuisance. Not safe, either, if you should have to get out in a hurry."

"Oh, I guess I'd never thought of that," Kara admitted. "Yes, I'll be around after school. If you're sure it's not too much trouble."

"No trouble at all."

He favored her with a smile that blotted out all but his commanding presence. Kara made a conscious effort to collect her scattered wits and slow the rapid beating of her heart. It was almost indecent the way the man affected her. And in her ungainly, bloated state! Her due date was less than a month away, and here she was, going all mushy inside over a man she barely knew.

Ever since Bric had walked into her classroom a few days ago, she'd been unable to get him out of her mind. There was something about his square-cut jaw and perceptive brown eyes that called to all that was female in her. Otherwise how could she account for the fact that just thinking about John Brickner made her pulse skip a beat? If he had any inkling that she was practically drooling over him—she with her stomach popping out in front—he would probably die laughing!

"When are we leaving, Mrs. Reynolds?" Billy piped up, jumping out of his seat in impatient enthusiasm.

It was all Kara could do to contain the hyperactive sixth grader. Any change in the daily routine worked on Billy like a shot of adrenaline. This time Kara was grateful that his fidgeting had interrupted her capricious musings. Suddenly she was conscious that four pairs of eyes were on her as she stood staring after Bric, who was depositing his tool kit on an empty desk.

With unsteady fingers, she hooked a strand of mahogany hair behind her ear. "In a few minutes," she promised. "Meanwhile, young man, sit back down and keep working on those story problems." She lumbered across the room and placed a firm hand on top of Billy's head until the seat of his pants made contact with the wooden chair.

She turned her attention to the rest of the class. "Ralph, you go over and see if you agree with the answers Ruth is getting to the problems on page fifty. Now, everybody back to work. If you children don't make good progress on today's assignments, we won't be able to take time to hunt for a tree."

When all heads were again bent in concentration, Kara walked toward Bric. In a quiet voice she confided, "I'm indulging in a bit of learning incentive today. Or I guess a more accurate term is bribery." She wrinkled her nose innocently. "When the children finish their lessons, we're going to look for a Christmas tree. Maybe you'd like to work on the door while we're out."

Bric solemnly studied her unwieldy gait as she drew closer. Had the woman taken leave of her senses? In her condition, she had no business trudging through the newly fallen snow. He scowled. "How are you planning to cut down a tree and get it back here? I don't see that teenage Hercules who was here the other day."

"Sam?" Pushing her way through the one free-swinging door, Kara motioned Bric into the school entrance, where their conversation wouldn't distract the children. "No, he and Delia go to high school on Middle Bass in the afternoons. I only have them for English and history, in the mornings. It works out nicely, since they can help me part of the day and then take the noon air shuttle to the island. The mail plane brings them back late in the afternoon."

As the door swished closed behind him, Bric inquired, "Who's chopping down the tree, then?" The lines in his brow deepened as he thought about the students he'd just been watching. Only the oldest looked big enough to wield an ax, but he was far too excitable and uncoordinated to be trusted with such a lethal weapon.

"I am, of course," Kara replied. Despite the fact that the double doors provided them with a modicum of privacy from prying ears, they were speaking in lowered voices. Their hushed tones and the narrow hall lined with coat hooks on one side and cabinets on the other side created an intimacy that made Kara decidedly uneasy.

"*You?* You're chopping down a Christmas tree? Have you looked at yourself in a mirror lately?" The words came out more forcefully than he'd intended.

Kara turned beet red. In rapid succession embarrassment, hurt, anger washed over her. She latched on to the anger. "There's no need to remind me that I'm very pregnant and ungraceful, Mr. Brickner," she bit out in an offended huff. "But my condition has not affected my brain, nor my ability to do mild forms of manual labor. I'm quite capable of cutting down a small tree and hauling it back to the school on a sled. As a child, I did just that with my father at least a dozen times."

"Hacking down a tree hardly qualifies as a mild form of exercise! There's no way I'm going to let you trot out in the snow to chop down a tree, little or not."

"What makes you think you can tell me what I can and can't do?" Kara blazed.

Immediately Bric cursed himself for a clumsy dolt. But he couldn't think clearly around her. All he knew was that she made him want to protect her, hover over her like a mother hen. But being a world-class jerk, he'd barreled ahead full steam without once considering her feelings. He'd embarrassed her by calling attention to her lack of grace and balance, by questioning her ability and judgment. And as if that weren't enough, he'd had the gall to challenge her independence. As if he had a right.

Trouble was, he wanted the right, wanted to be in control. And that need had made him overly assertive. What was wrong with him, anyway? Had one painful experience warped him forever? Or did he react that way because even pregnant Kara was more beautiful than any woman had a right to be?

Bric rubbed the back of his neck. "I'm sorry. I only thought . . . that is, I'd be glad to chop down a tree for you *and* plane this door."

He looked so contrite that Kara softened in spite of herself. "That's kind of you. But pregnant woman aren't helpless, Mr. Brickner."

"They have no business chopping down trees." The stubborn set to his jaw brooked no argument.

A slow smile stole across Kara's face. "I intended for it to be a very small tree. However, since you offer so nicely—" she emphasized the last word "—you're welcome to come along."

As soon as the invitation left her mouth, she regretted it. Her mounded belly was a telling reminder of how recently she'd vowed to steer clear of the male of the species. Still, she rationalized, accepting a small favor wasn't tantamount to letting John Brickner into her life. And she couldn't fault his reasoning. A woman more than eight months pregnant shouldn't be hiking through the woods to fell a Christmas tree.

"Thank you," she said, brushing a loose lock of hair off her forehead.

Bric suddenly longed to reach out and sift the silky mass of burnished copper through his fingers. Instead, he stuck his hands into his back pockets and, in a voice gone slightly husky, insisted, "My pleasure."

The way he looked at her had Kara's blood humming. To hide her confusion, she excused herself in a hoarse whisper that sounded strained even to her ears. Back in the classroom, she checked each child's paper, then announced that they could get ready to go outside.

Bric cleared the entry and stood just within the room as laughing children located boots, scarves, coats and hats. He lounged against the doorjamb, smiling at the confusion and excitement. Their wholesome chatter brought to mind his own happy childhood at the same time that it sent a sharp pang of regret chasing through him.

Supposedly time healed all wounds, but Elaine's betrayal was something he'd never forget. Every time her image flashed before him, he felt what he'd promised himself he'd never feel again.

Swallowing the hurtful memory, Bric watched Joey's inept struggles with high-topped rubber galoshes and fought an inclination to help him tug them on. But when he saw Kara sit on her desk chair and stiffly bend over to remove her shoes in favor of fur-lined boots, he bolted forward. "Let me."

Kara's laugh was a compelling sound that wrapped him in a sudden warmth. Warmth and something more he didn't care to analyze at the moment.

"It takes a while, but I can do it."

"No sense keeping the kids waiting. They're ready to burst through those doors right now." He nodded toward the jostling youngsters, who were dutifully scrambling into a haphazard line.

"Very well. But I warn you, I could get used to being taken care of, and I might prove demanding." Her teasing tone was meant to ease the mesmeric pull Bric exerted as he hunkered down and lifted one stockinged foot. Yet at the merest brush of his fingers on her ankle, she recoiled as if branded.

"Are my hands still cold?" He propped her foot on his taut thigh and rapidly rubbed his palms together.

"No, it's all right," she assured him, acutely aware of her heel resting on his leg.

With swift, easy movements, he slipped her feet into the boots, then helped her on with her coat. It barely buttoned over her high stomach, but Bric was intrigued by the fetching picture Kara made as she wrapped a red scarf around her neck and pulled a ski cap on her head. "All ready, Mr. Brickner," she pronounced as she drew on matching knit gloves.

"Now that I've helped bundle you up, don't you think we know each other well enough for you to call me Bric?" Casually he cupped her elbow and led her toward the door.

"My name's Kara," she said by way of reply.

"I'll remember that . . . Teacher."

Kara shot him a sidelong glance. "Eavesdropper," she charged, giving him a flippant toss of her head.

* * *

Excited squeals erupted when Ralph and Ruth spied a nearly symmetrical blue spruce in a wooded area that needed thinning.

"This one! This one!" they shouted.

Motioning everyone out of harm's way, Bric circled the tree to decide where to take his first swing. Kara stood, entranced, as, feet astride, he lifted the ax and swung at the trunk, the muscles of his back working effortlessly beneath the leather of his flight jacket. All the while, the children jumped up and down, shouting and clapping their mittened hands, their high voices mingling with the sharp ring of steel against wood.

After downing the spruce with a minimum of strokes, Bric secured it to Billy's sled. Taking turns, the youngsters paired off to pull the tree back to the schoolhouse. When Joey yanked so hard he fell over backward, Bric salved his pride by swooping the small boy onto his shoulders and carrying him the rest of the way.

Joey's happy face brought a smile to Kara's lips. That Bric was sensitive enough to recognize the child's wounded ego touched her profoundly. With a feeling close to envy, she watched Joey wrap his small fingers around Bric's solid jaw and found herself wondering what it would be like to trace its beard-shadowed contour with her fingertips.

Pushing the unbidden picture from her thoughts, Kara directed her attention to Ruth. The little girl was hanging on to her arm, miffed that Ralph and Billy had taken charge of the sled.

"On Monday we'll pop a huge bowl of corn and string a garland. It'll go fast with all of us working," Kara promised.

"We never got to do that before," Ruth bubbled. "You're the best teacher in the world!"

When Bric caught her eye and smiled, Kara felt the color deepen on her already wind-reddened cheeks.

Two hours later Kara was measuring butter and salt into a Revere Ware pot and adjusting the electric burner. Carpentry sounds drew her gaze through the open door of her apartment into the adjoining schoolroom, where the regal blue-green spruce stood ready to be trimmed.

Hands braced at the base of her spine, she arched her aching back. It had been an especially exhausting day, but she wouldn't have traded its simple pleasures for anything. Slowly she walked through the kitchen door and stopped before the four-foot tree, its fresh pine fragrance scenting the air with the promise of Christmas. Already she could picture the handmade ornaments that would add color to the graceful branches. Again she pressed her hands against the small of her back and stretched.

"Tired?" a low voice from behind asked.

She turned to find Bric smiling at her.

"That's the second time today I didn't hear you come up behind me. What are you, part Indian?"

"Jungle warfare," he confessed, an icy remoteness momentarily hardening the dark brown of his eyes. "I was in Vietnam."

"Oh." Her intonation conveyed a wealth of meaning. Sympathy. Respect. Understanding. Gratitude.

"I flew helicopters, so I didn't see much ground action." Quickly he changed the subject. "I'm all finished with your door. It shouldn't give you any more trouble."

As a range of emotions played across his face, Kara watched, fascinated by their depth and complexity. For the space of a heartbeat, silence hung between them. She rapidly collected herself. "You've been very kind to us. How can we repay you?"

He cocked his head toward the kitchen, drawing in a long, appreciative sniff. "There are some tantalizing aromas floating in here. Almost sinful, in fact. Especially to a bachelor who's an indifferent cook."

Kara laughed as much in amusement at the overt hint as in relief that the tension had passed. "How thoughtless of me! Of course, you must be starved after chopping down that tree and repairing our door. I'd be pleased if you stayed for supper."

When he smiled, tiny lines radiated from the corners of his eyes. "Not as pleased as I am to accept."

"Better reserve your compliments until after you taste my cooking," she countered, leading the way to her apartment.

"If it tastes half as good as it smells, I'll think I died and went to heaven."

During the meal, Kara learned that Bric had grown up with two brothers and two sisters, that all were married except for him and that after Vietnam he'd established his own aviation service with a marine buddy. It came as no surprise to her that he enjoyed working with wood, a skill he'd picked up from his father.

For his part, Bric found out that Kara's parents lived in Cincinnati, where her father was a professor of political science and her mother a partner in a prominent law firm.

As if by tacit agreement, they both kept to safe subjects until Bric wondered aloud, "Is that where you lived with your husband—Cincinnati?"

"Yes." Her gaze dropped to her lap. "He was on Mother's legal staff."

"I see." Though Bric was curious about what had happened to Kara's husband, he didn't want to probe. "Well, I've never had a more satisfying meal! Or a more delicious one!"

"Thank you, but it's probably the cold air." Kara put down her cup, braced both elbows on the table and rested her chin on folded hands. "With your appetite, I could probably have served toasted cardboard and you wouldn't have complained!"

"Was my gluttony that obvious? I've probably demolished your week's supply of groceries."

"More like two days' worth," she said, a twinkle in her eyes.

"Sorry." Bric grinned, looking anything but. "I promise to make it up to you with the very next grocery delivery I fly in."

"Please, it was little enough for all you did." She added frankly, "And for the pleasant company."

Bric reached across the table and claimed one of her hands. As he cradled her fingers in his work-roughened palms, Kara felt blanketed in a comforting warmth.

"Why did you come here, Kara? An isolated island in Lake Erie isn't the ideal location for a widow who's about to have a baby."

Widow! The word slammed through Kara like a jolt of electricity. She'd never said anything about being widowed!

Kara reclaimed her hand and sifted through their previous conversations. Finally it came to her. She remembered having told Bric she'd "lost" Edmund. What she'd failed to add was "to another woman."

It was on the tip of Kara's tongue to confess she was divorced, but the words caught in her throat. The subject was too painful, the wound too fresh, to discuss with someone she scarcely knew.

Besides, she rationalized, what harm was there in Bric's thinking Edmund was dead? As far as she was concerned, he might as well be. After the abominable way he'd behaved, if she never laid eyes on the man for the rest of her life, it would be too soon.

"I've done it again, haven't I?" Bric asked.

Kara came out of her reverie. "I beg your pardon?"

"This seems to be my day for putting my foot in my mouth. I didn't mean to imply you've done the wrong thing. I was just curious about how you ended up on Perry's."

"Because I got a job here," she answered matter-of-factly.

Bric tilted his empty water glass, turning it reflectively in one hand. "But there are jobs on the mainland, closer to your family and friends. With your qualifications, surely you could've had your pick."

"Perhaps." Kara lowered her gaze to the table. "But I didn't start looking until mid-August. By then most positions were filled. And my condition didn't help."

Bric clamped flattened palms over his thighs to subdue an urge to gather her in his arms. He'd never been so immediately attracted to a woman before, and certainly never one eight months pregnant. For some reason the male in him wanted to care for her. Maybe it was instinctive—this need to protect an expectant mother who had no husband—or maybe it was a natural reaction, given his own problem, but somehow he didn't think either reason adequate for the strong feelings Kara Reynolds aroused in him. Time and again she pulled at him as no woman ever had. Certainly not Elaine. Not even Gloria, the only other woman he'd come close to marrying.

"I hadn't thought of that," he admitted.

The touch of self-criticism in his tone brought Kara's head up. For one heart-stopping moment, she stared directly into his penetrating brown eyes. Then her attention shifted to the faint scar etched across the curve of Bric's right cheekbone. Instantly she had to quell an unreasonable desire to trace it with a fingertip.

She settled for running an index finger around the rim of her cup. "It wasn't as if I had no support. Actually I had too much." She shrugged indifferently. "My parents tend to be overprotective. Only-child syndrome, I guess."

"I'm not much for coddling, either. After I was mustered out of the service, I got my fill of pampering." More than enough to last a lifetime, Bric thought with distaste. Despite a rapid physical recovery, it had taken him a good two years to regain some semblance of emotional stability. But, he admitted miserably, there were some parts of him that would never mend.

What about Kara? Obviously she had some battle scars of her own. While she toyed with her cup, Bric took time to study her. Except for the swell of her abdomen, she looked far too thin for her height. About five foot six, he gauged, thinking that the top of her head would barely come to his shoulder. He wondered how she was going to manage alone on this sparsely populated island once her child was born.

Breaking the brief silence, he asked, "How much maternity leave will you get?"

Kara brightened. "About a month. I'm due around the holidays, so I won't have to be out of the classroom long. Then Delia's mother will sit for me. Since she does a lot of needlecraft for a shop in Port Clinton, she's agreed to bring her work along and take care of the baby right here at the apartment. It's an ideal arrangement, really.''

"Except for one thing." He paused meaningfully. "What about a social life? You won't find much here."

"Enough," Kara insisted, giving herself a cumbersome shove from the table. "And the island's a nice place for a young child."

Almost simultaneously Bric scraped back his wooden chair. "You rest," he directed. "I'm no great shakes as a chef, but my talent for scrubbing pots goes unchallenged."

Smiling, Kara stacked their plates and carried them to the kitchen. "So your parents made you boys help wash dishes, huh?"

"Often. Besides, I drew my share of KP in the service. Believe me, after that, this is a snap."

"If you say so." She turned from placing the dishes in the sink and bumped solidly into Bric. Flinching as if scalded, she mumbled an apology and stepped back, only to find herself trapped between him and the counter.

Bric put his arms out to steady her. Her beautifully translucent complexion made her seem as breakable as fine china. He slid his hands to her back and pulled her to him. "Are you all right?"

Kara felt herself go limp. How good it was to be held against a strong body. Gratefully she nestled her head against the hollow of his throat and let her arms encircle his waist. A faint hint of pine blended with something spicy, something all-male, to tantalize her senses. She breathed deeply of it.

Her moist breath fanned the coils of hair exposed by his open-necked shirt, sending a shiver rocking through him. It seemed only natural that he clasp her more tightly.

For a long moment they stood motionless, locked in each other's arms. Then, without warning, something nudged Bric. At first he believed Kara was pushing him away. But her head still rested lightly under his chin, her breath still teased the crisp hair beneath his throat and her slender arms still encircled his waist. When he felt the jostle again, a definite thump against his midsection, he squeezed his eyes shut, overpowered by an unexpected sensation.

The baby's kicking roused Kara, and she lifted her head to lean back. "Sorry," she murmured, flushing when she became aware of the intimacy of their embrace. "I don't know what came over me. Dizzy, I guess."

"Don't apologize. I liked holding you. And the baby." His voice was roughened with feeling. "I never felt a baby move before."

Looking up into his eyes, Kara was met by a vulnerability that surprised her. She was touched by the awe, the wonder gentling his features. Unhesitatingly she lifted his hand and placed it over her stomach. As if on cue, the baby pushed against his large palm.

Tentatively Bric curled his fingers around what felt like the sole of a tiny foot. For an instant he allowed himself to pretend it was the child he'd lost that stirred against his flesh.

Kara tilted her head down. "When she first moved, it felt like the flutter of a butterfly's wings. Now she's getting more aggressive. Sometimes I think she'll be a lady boxer."

"She?" Bric repeated, reluctantly withdrawing his hand. "You're positive it's a girl?"

"No, but I hope it's a girl. A boy would need a father more. To teach him ... boy things."

"So you don't have a throwing arm?"

Kara smiled, grateful he'd lightened the tension. "Among other things."

Laughing, Bric observed, "If you do have a boy, it'll be a while before you have to worry about that. Now, you relax while I get to work on these dishes."

Kara let Bric install her on the sofa and prop her ankles on a footstool. True to his word, he washed and dried the dishes and left the cooking area spotless. By the time he'd finished, she was half-asleep, her head tilted back against the plump cushions.

"Sure you'll be all right?" he asked as he wiped his hands on a towel and hung it beside the sink.

Her eyes opened. "Of course."

He wasn't convinced. "That long walk was probably too much for you."

"Nonsense. It was just what the doctor ordered."

Bric shifted his weight from one leg to the other. Though he no longer had an excuse to linger, he was reluctant to leave. "I put the number of my plane service and my private number by your phone. No matter what time of day or night, call me. I'll be here in a half hour, tops."

"I'm sure you have more important things to do than worry about me. Don't you know first babies usually take a long time to get themselves born?"

"Since I'm providing taxi service, I'd appreciate plenty of advance notice." The comment brought a laugh from Kara. "Can I do anything else for you before I go?"

"Not a thing. Sometime, though, I would like to fly to the mainland for some shopping. I haven't much of what I'll be needing for the baby. Only a few essentials Mother sent. I've got to buy a crib yet and some more blankets for sure. I'd like to combine the trip with one of my visits to the doctor. If you could lend me a car, I'd appreciate it."

"You name the time, and I'll see you get one. After you finish shopping, we'll have lunch at my favorite café. I owe you a couple of meals for what I put away tonight." As he picked up his jacket, Kara swung her feet to the floor and started to lever herself off the sofa. Bric held out a staying hand. "Don't get up. I can let myself out."

"You more than earned your dinner, Bric." Kara paused before adding, "It's been a nice evening."

On impulse he walked over and bent close. "I've enjoyed it, too." His lips coasted so lightly over her forehead that Kara wasn't sure if she had only imagined the gentle touch of his mouth.

With that, he turned and quickly strode out the door.

Chapter Three

Kara held up the yellow terry sleeper and smiled. So tiny, she mused. Hardly big enough, even for a doll. With loving care she folded the little garment and placed it alongside the gowns, undershirts and receiving blankets she'd purchased that morning.

As promised, Bric had flown her to the mainland so she could finish her shopping. Kara hadn't meant to postpone completing the layette, but when she'd first come to Perry's Island, her baby's arrival had seemed such a long way off. Once she'd solved the problem of finding an obstetrician, she'd gotten so caught up in getting organized for the different grades she would be teaching that before she'd known it, school had started and fall had quietly slipped into winter. Without her so much as turning around, or so it seemed.

Kara smoothed the miniature togs and closed her dresser drawer. For some reason her stomach was lodging an almost queasy protest. All the excitement of the day, she imagined. Or maybe Baby thought it was time to eat again.

As she wandered into the narrow kitchen, Kara patted her belly. "Already starting to get demanding, aren't you, precious?" For answer, she was rewarded with a resounding kick. "Okay, okay, we'll eat," she cajoled, opening the refrigerator door. "But you shouldn't be so grouchy after that enormous lunch Bric treated us to."

The thought of Bric kindled a warm glow that left Kara just a mite breathless. Not entirely certain she welcomed the response, she began a haphazard search through an assortment of leftovers.

True, she conceded, Bric's rugged good looks were enough to turn any woman's head. But what really gave her pause was something that went deeper than mere surface appeal. Beneath his rough exterior and hard planes, she'd glimpsed a sensitivity that was both unanticipated and endearing. It was that more than anything that moved her.

Kara's mouth curved into a tender smile as she recalled how Bric had insisted on accompanying her while she shopped. She'd expected him to hand over the car keys and arrange to meet her later. Instead, he'd insisted upon waiting in the parking lot while she kept her doctor's appointment, then had driven her around to every baby shop and department from Sandusky to Port Clinton. Not only that, but he had helped her decide on a crib, later carted it to her apartment and even assembled it before hauling in a fresh supply of wood for school on Monday morning. At least, she breathed in relief, she'd convinced him to head back in time to beat the snow squall. What had started as idle flurries showed every sign of turning into a major winter storm.

From her refrigerator Kara lifted a carton of milk and the remnants of a roast. As she bumped the door closed with a hip, she remembered how one of the salesgirls that afternoon had mistaken her and Bric for a couple. Kara could feel again the fiery blush that had heated her face. She could have died of embarrassment, but Bric hadn't seemed one whit disturbed. He'd laughingly agreed with the clerk that becoming a parent was the most exciting thing in the world. To emphasize his point, he'd circled her waist and spread his wide palm possessively over her abdomen.

When Kara had momentarily stiffened at the public intimacy, Bric had withdrawn his hand, but not without caressing her warmly as he skimmed it down her side and over her thigh. Slipping out of his grasp, she had looked up to catch an unreadable expression in his dark eyes. If she hadn't known better, she would have sworn Bric had been hurt by her retreat.

Dimly, Kara wondered what it would be like if Bric was her baby's father. How would it have been if he'd made love to her? She caught herself imagining what it would be like to run her hands over the swell of his firm muscles, to trace the contours of his finely sculpted mouth with the tip of her tongue, to . . .

With an impatient shake of her head, Kara swept the sensual image from her mind. What was she doing, leaning against her refrigerator and mooning over John Brickner? Her marriage should have cured her of any romantic notions left over from a naive girlhood, a time when she had mistakenly believed she could attract a man, marry him and live happily ever after. Hadn't Edmund taught her just how lacking in appeal she was? And that was before pregnancy had transformed her into an unwieldy elephant.

As Kara turned to lower the remains of her roast to the counter, the milk carton slipped from her fingers, its contents splattering floor and cabinets. When she stooped to blot up the mess, a severe pain twisted through her middle, bending her double. "No, it can't be," she objected.

With her hands clutched around her stomach, Kara slid down the side of the counter. "Not tonight. Not in this storm."

Bric sat with his feet propped on a rolltop desk stacked high with the paperwork he'd neglected for the past several days. Normally the desk was swept clear, its polished wood gleaming like the frozen surface of Lake Erie in winter.

He hated paperwork, preferring the freedom of flying the company's Cessna 185s and 270s. But running an airline, even one as small as Erie Islands, required attention to detail. Though his partner, Mark Carlisle, was more than willing to shoulder his share of the work, there was always plenty to keep Bric busy. And so, day in, day out, he had forced himself to put in the hours necessary to keep a step ahead of all the correspondence and reports.

He'd managed quite well until about two weeks ago, when he'd had his first glimpse of an auburn-haired, violet-eyed beauty. Since then, about the only thing he'd accomplished in the office was to sit around, shuffling papers from one pile to another.

Bric snorted disgustedly. He knew damn well it was a mistake even to *think* about her, let alone entertain notions of getting involved. But no matter how hard he tried, he couldn't push visions of Kara Reynolds out of his head.

The coiled spring supporting the seat of his chair complained loudly as Bric's feet hit the floor. Bracing himself with a fortifying intake of air, he picked up a letter dated November 27.

Before he had a chance to finish skimming the latest Federal Aviation Administration directive, the muffled jangle of his phone broke into his concentration. He located the cord, which disappeared under a heap of paper, and yanked. "Brickner," he barked into the receiver, irritated that he had yet to go through a single piece of paperwork.

Bric could barely make out the strained voice at the other end of a line popping with static. "Kara, is that you?" he asked, not at all certain his mind wasn't playing tricks on him. He jerked the phone away from his ear as electronic hisses and spits crackled over the wire. "Kara? What's wrong?"

"The baby... I think it's coming."

A cold shiver of panic fragmented Kara's reply and stabbed at his insides. *Oh, God, not tonight,* he prayed, swiveling toward the window and eyeing what looked like showers of confetti in a ticker-tape parade. "Isn't it too early?"

"Tell that to the baby." A brittle laugh died in Kara's throat. "Bric... oh, Bric. This blizzard... I'm scared."

His stomach tightened into a hard knot. "Kara, honey, hang on." Pinching the receiver between shoulder and jaw, he lunged for his flight jacket and began working his arms into the sleeves. "Call Mrs. McCann. She'll know what to do. I'll need every available car on the island lined up with its lights aimed at the landing strip."

Bric realized he was shouting, that his rapid-fire instructions might upset her. But he couldn't help it. "I'm on my way," he tried to reassure her, then banged down the phone and burst out the door.

For Bric the past sixty minutes had seemed more like sixty years. Even though the cockpit of the Cessna couldn't have been warmer than fifty degrees, a film of sweat beaded his forehead. He called on every ounce of control he could muster to keep from shouting his frustration and voicing his fear that the wings might ice up. Just reaching the island in this mess had been bad enough. Having to take off again in it had been pushing his luck.

Bric took his gaze away from the swirling snow long enough to glimpse at the woman beside him. Her eyes were closed, her arms wrapped protectively around her middle. He could tell she was riding out a strong contraction. A string of blistering curses fell from his lips as he leaned closer to the Plexiglass windscreen and squinted into the storm. By now visibility was down to about a mile, and he had to depend mostly on instruments and instinct.

A muffled groan from Kara had him feeling for her hand. "I radioed ahead for an ambulance. Only a little while longer," he said soothingly, hoping he spoke the truth.

Kara opened her eyes and focused on his profile. So strong, dependable, capable. She knew the danger she and Bric were in. The small plane was being buffeted about as if it were no more substantial than a balsawood toy. The motion did nothing for her equilibrium, neither emotionally nor physically. Especially now that the pains were coming closer and closer together. That last one had felt as though the baby meant business.

She gave the fingers that held hers a tight squeeze. "It's okay. I'm a little airsick, that's all. Have I gotten us into a lot of trouble?"

Bric clasped her hand more firmly. Fear had long ago replaced panic, but he wouldn't allow himself to give in to it. "Trouble? Who said anything about trouble?"

"Certainly not you." The beginning of a smile faded on her lips as she was swept by another wave of pain. "Maybe," she offered after it had passed, "I should have stayed home and let Mrs. McCann play midwife." Her hand slipped from his to brush a damp tendril away from her face.

"No way. If this baby insists on rushing his birth date, he's going to get himself born in a hospital."

"She," Kara amended pointedly, pressing flattened palms on either side of her legs and pushing back in her seat. "Two weeks early, that's hardly premature."

"No sense in taking any chances," Bric insisted. At once he was struck by the irony of his words. If flying on a night like this wasn't taking a chance, he didn't know what was, but he kept his tone level. "Now, stop worrying. Everything's going to work out fine. Believe me, I've flown in lots worse," he lied.

One corner of her mouth slanted in a wry smile. "Are you always this honest?"

"Count on it." Bric forced his face into a carefree grin, but his body was attuned to the drone of the engine and the whine of the wind. He couldn't name the moment when Kara Reynolds had slipped past all those defenses he'd been so careful to erect through the years. All he knew was that she'd become more important to him than any woman had ever been. And he wasn't about to allow anything to happen to her...or to her baby. Yes, by God, he vowed, this was one baby he wasn't going to lose! Bric concentrated his full attention on the bank of instruments that kept the Cessna on course. Where the hell was the airfield, anyway? By this time he should have been able to pick up the string of lights along the runway.

He was beginning to think he'd miscalculated when he spied Cedar Point Peninsula. For the first time since the bush plane had thundered down the graveled strip at Perry's Island, Bric allowed himself a deep, steadying breath. Sandusky Municipal Airport was only a few miles south of the peninsula.

He eased back on the throttle and lowered the wing flaps. The plane responded with a decrease of speed and a corresponding drop in altitude. Soon the snow-covered ground was coming up to meet them. Bric closed down the throttle and gently pulled back on the stick a split second before the front wheels settled with a bump on the tarmac.

Three hours later Bric was twisting on a hard vinyl chair and absently patting his shirt pocket before he remembered that he'd quit smoking a year ago. What he'd give for a cigarette now! This waiting was driving him crazy. Nervously he checked his watch and was astonished to discover that it was not yet midnight. Why did it seem like days since he'd landed the Cessna in a swirl of blinding snow and turned Kara over to the medical team at the waiting ambulance?

The inveterate pacer with whom he shared the hospital waiting room wasn't making matters easier. The young man alternated between fidgeting in a chair and prowling the small lounge.

In desperate need of diversion, Bric pulled some change from his pocket and strode to the coffee machine. While steaming liquid poured into the cup, he turned to his lone companion. "First baby?"

"How'd you know?"

Bric smiled. "Lucky guess."

"You're so calm, you must be an old hand at this."

"Not exactly," Bric offered noncommittally. Did he really appear that cool and collected? If he did, maybe he should change his profession and give acting a whirl. It had to be a hell of a lot less dangerous. Grinning crookedly, he lifted the plastic door and retrieved his black coffee.

"Name's Halliday, Gene Halliday." The man wiped his damp palms on his thighs and stuck out a long hand.

"John Brickner. Want some coffee?" He held out the untouched cup.

"No, I'm keyed up enough. How much longer is it going to be, anyhow? She's been in labor ever since last night."

"The first ones take longer," Bric assured the man, remembering that Kara had told him first babies were usually a while in coming. Still, hers had seemed in a big hurry. He knew that by the time they'd landed, her contractions were only a few minutes apart.

"I wish I had agreed to those natural childbirth classes. But I didn't think I could take it," the younger man confessed. "Afraid I'd faint at the sight of blood. You decided against them, too, huh?"

"Hmm," Bric murmured over a sip of coffee. Had he fathered Kara's child, he'd have made damn sure to have whatever training he needed to go through the baby's birth with her. As far as he was concerned, any man who didn't want to witness the birth of his own child was an out-and-out fool. But then, Halliday looked not much more than a kid himself.

"You want a girl or boy?" Halliday asked.

"She wants a girl."

"I don't care. Long as it's healthy. And long as it gets here soon."

Just then a friendly-looking nurse came through the door. "Mr. Halliday, you have a beautiful baby boy."

"A boy! Did you hear that?" he asked, giving Bric a hearty slap on the back before turning toward the nurse. "How's Marlene?"

"Your wife's doing fine. She's a little tired right now, but you can see her in a few minutes. Follow me and I'll introduce you to your son."

With a twinge of envy, Bric congratulated Halliday. He downed the last of his coffee, then tossed the empty cup in the trash. Why was he waiting around, anyway? After he'd found Kara's insurance card in her wallet and officially admitted her, he'd been free to leave. Hell, it wasn't his baby, and they probably wouldn't even let him see it. Still, he couldn't desert her at a time like this. Couldn't, or didn't want to? he upbraided himself.

Bric settled back on the chair, turning over and over in his mind their frantic arrival at the hospital. He'd felt like a snoop going through Kara's purse for answers to questions put to him by the admitting clerk. With a grimace he wondered why he hadn't been able to stop himself from shuffling through some snapshots encased in a clear plastic folder. Was it simple curiosity or something more complex that had him violating her privacy in search of a picture of her dead husband? It was unlike Bric to stick his nose where it didn't belong, and he chided himself for what he considered a breach of trust. Surprisingly, he hadn't found a single picture of a man. Only grinning faces of schoolchildren greeted him from behind the glossy inserts.

"Mr. Brickner?"

With a start, Bric jumped out of his seat. "Is everything all right?" he asked the nurse who had led Halliday away only thirty minutes earlier.

"Yes. I thought you'd like to know that Mrs. Reynolds is fine. She has a healthy baby girl."

At the news, tension rushed from his tautly strung body like air from a suddenly punctured balloon. "Is there anything she needs? Anything I can do?"

"You can ask her yourself. She refused any anesthetic, so she's wide-awake and very excited. Come on. I'll take you to her room."

Kara was propped up in bed, her long tresses spilling over the white pillow like a fine cloud of spun copper. In the soft hospital light, her pale features radiated happiness. A dainty bundle was nestled snugly in her arms. When Bric stepped through the door, Kara looked up and fairly bubbled, "Isn't she beautiful?"

Bric walked over to the bed and forced himself not to imagine that the three of them were a family. "Just like her mother. And just what you wanted. A little girl." With a gentle motion he brushed aside the soft blanket and tipped his head to study the infant. She had an incredibly small nose and mouth and an amazing amount of silky brown hair. A perfectly formed little hand, complete with rather long fingernails, inched its way out of the covers. He couldn't resist a tender impulse to lift the minuscule fingers with one of his own.

Kara's eyes glistened with joy. "I already called Mother and Dad. They'll be here tomorrow. That is, if the roads have been cleared. What time is it, anyway?"

Carefully Bric lowered the tiny hand and glanced at his watch. "A little after one. It didn't take her very long, once she decided to make her debut. But I can't say much for the little lady's sense of timing. She sure picked the worst night of the year."

When the baby yawned, Bric was overwhelmed by a sense of protectiveness. He reached out and ran a knuckle down her pink cheek.

"You want to hold her?"

Bric swallowed. "I'm not sure I know how."

"All you have to do is make a cradle of your arms and support her head. Sit down and see what she feels like."

Bric sank to the edge of the bed and almost reverently took Kara's daughter into his arms. "She's as light as a feather," he marveled, emotion swelling in his throat. "What will you name her?"

"Lynda Joan. Lynda comes from the Spanish word for 'lovely,' while the Christian meaning of Joan is 'gift of the Lord.' But I'll call her Lynn."

Bric thought of another baby, another time, and something knotted inside him. Kara was so loving and giving—unlike Elaine, who had refused to marry him and then, without bothering to ask, aborted their child. All that had happened long ago, when he was a boy of eighteen. If his baby had lived, he thought, he or she would be eighteen now.

With one large, blunt-edged finger he tickled the tip of Lynn's chin. "It's a perfect name for her. I'd say you got yourself quite a Christmas present."

Maybe Lynn was a gift for him, too, he mused. In a way, this baby had given him a chance to experience something that had been taken away from him. But he shouldn't become too attached to her. She wasn't his child, he brutally reminded himself. Yet given how he felt about her mother, he had to acknowledge a small hope lingering at the back of his mind.

With the utmost care Bric lowered Lynn into Kara's arms. "You'd better be getting some sleep. I don't suppose there's any need to notify the school board that you'll be out until after the holidays. I don't think there was a car on Perry's that wasn't there to light up the airstrip."

"Quite a dramatic send-off, wasn't it?" Kara laughed and sought his hand. "Thanks, Bric. For both of us."

"Oh, excuse me." A nurse poked her head inside the door.

"I was just leaving," Bric said.

"I don't want to rush you. Fathers have rights, too," the nurse gushed.

Not according to Elaine, Bric thought painfully as he said his goodbyes and exited the room.

"Mr. Reynolds," the nurse called, stopping him midway down the hall.

Bric turned abruptly, ready to explain that he wasn't Kara's husband, but the woman hurrying toward him jabbered on. "I was in the delivery room with your wife, and I wanted to tell you, she's real brave and sweet. For a first baby, Mrs. Reynolds had a pretty easy time. You wouldn't think it to look at her, but she's sure built to have babies." The woman laid a hand on his arm and finished with a confidential wink. "Good thing, too, since she said she'd like lots of them."

Her words cut through Bric like a steel blade. "Exactly what I wanted to hear," he said coldly, bringing a puzzled frown to the nurse's face. He wheeled around and headed down the hospital corridor, his features contorted in a tight mask. With unnecessary force, he punched the elevator button for the bottom floor. He should have known better. Kara loved children. That was one reason she was such a good teacher. But since she had all those kids at school and since she'd been an only child, he'd foolishly thought... He checked himself, refusing to rehash his own faulty reasoning. Well, he'd see to it that she got some flowers, and he'd pilot her and the baby safely home. But then he'd back off.

What rotten luck! Bric slammed down the hospital steps. At thirty-seven, when it was too late, he'd found a woman he could build a life with, a woman who aroused feelings he'd thought dead. And she wanted the one thing he could never give her.

Chapter Four

Kara bloused her royal-blue lamb's wool dress over a wide leather belt, then critically surveyed the results. "Not bad," she assured her image as she adjusted the cuffs on the raglan sleeves and slowly turned for a better view in the full-length mirror. Pressing a hand to her stomach, she eyed her profile. "Not bad at all for the mother of a six-week-old daughter," she pronounced. Softly gathered at the waist, the sweater dress camouflaged the slack muscles she was still firming with daily exercise.

She opened two neckline buttons and spread the collar to reveal a single pearl dangling from a thin gold chain. Satisfied that she'd pass muster, she suddenly wondered why it mattered so much. Personal pride, she told herself. She wanted to look her best at Delia and Sam's wedding. Besides, a sparsely populated island didn't offer all that many occasions to dress up.

Briefly, Kara reflected on why Sam and Delia had moved up their marriage date. Although no one had said, she suspected there was a baby on the way. If so, perhaps she could help prepare the couple for the responsibility of parenthood. A wry smile lifted her lips at the prospect of adding "family living" to her already crowded curriculum.

A lusty cry intruded into Kara's musings and drew her to the other side of the bedroom.

"Hungry, love?" She bent over the crib and offered her daughter soothing pats. "Your bottle's almost ready."

As Kara set in motion the colorful mobile attached to the crib, Lynn's large cornflower-blue eyes seemed to follow the nursery-rhyme figures dancing above her head.

Kara watched her daughter's tiny arms and legs move in an aimless expression of joy. What a comfort and blessing Lynn was! No matter what painful resentment she harbored against her ex-husband, Kara couldn't fault him for having given her this precious baby.

Lately she'd begun to question her decision not to tell Edmund about their child. When he'd asked for a divorce, pride had prevented her from trying to hold on to him with the news of her pregnancy. Was pride still keeping her silent? Perhaps, Kara conceded. After all this time, Edmund was bound to think she was only after money. And she couldn't bear to have him believe that, when she was perfectly capable of supporting Lynn herself.

As Kara smiled lovingly down at her daughter, a fresh doubt assailed her. Was there a trace of revenge in her silence? Was she trying to get back at her ex-husband by denying him the joys of fatherhood? The possibility that she might be using their child as a weapon gave her pause. Even Kara's parents, who by no stretch of the imagination condoned Edmund's conduct, had voiced their concern.

As if Lynn could intuit her mother's thoughts, the infant screwed up her face and bellowed for all she was worth.

"There, there, I get the message," Kara reproved with gentle tolerance. "It's bottle time."

After protecting her shoulder with a burp cloth, she tested the temperature of the formula and settled into a rocker. As Lynn ate greedily, Kara experienced a twinge of disappointment that she'd been unable to nurse longer. Once back in the classroom, however, she'd been hard-pressed to juggle her baby's erratic mealtimes with the demands of teaching. Nonetheless, she considered herself lucky. Not many working mothers were able to see their children during the day, let alone hold them during their lunch hour. Contentedly she let her head drop against the back of the rocker.

Outside the bedroom window, snow adorned the limbs of a lone spruce. Every time Kara looked at the tree, she was reminded of Bric. "I wonder what he'd think of you now," she said to the baby.

And why should you care? she berated herself. After Bric had flown her and Lynn back to the island and turned them over to her parents, he'd virtually disappeared. She didn't like to admit that his avoiding her and the baby hurt, but hardly a day went by that he didn't invade her thoughts.

Gently she withdrew the bottle and tipped Lynn over her shoulder. As she patted the baby's back, Kara decided that she was being oversensitive about the man because he'd happened to share with her the most important event in her life. Maybe pregnancy had heightened her sensitivities, tricking her into imagining that he felt something more than kindhearted concern.

Again she pillowed Lynn in her arms and continued the feeding. She had to put John Brickner out of her mind. Handsome as he was, he must have scores of females competing for his attentions. Why should he care about a woman with a baby? Why would he want to be saddled with another man's child?

All the same, Kara would never forget the tender look on Bric's face when she'd placed his palm over the rounded swell of her abdomen. Or the solemn way he'd touched and then held Lynn in the hospital.

Again shifting the infant to her shoulder, Kara checked the time. "Well, Lynnie, think you can give me another burp? It won't be long before Joey's aunt and uncle come to take us to the church."

While Kara changed the baby's diaper and slipped her into a pink sweater, she carried on a continuous chatter. "The McCanns and Linskeys are flying some guests over from the mainland today, so I want to see your best party manners. Got that, missy?"

Kara was planting a soft kiss on Lynn's forehead when a horn beeped for them outside.

Bric was the last person Kara expected to find among the wedding guests but the first she confronted as she emerged from the Parkers' station wagon. He was sliding open the door of a van parked just in front of them. As his gaze clung to hers, his features were darkened by a scowl, the same brooding expression he'd given her that first day in the classroom.

How astonishing, she reflected, that she seemed to draw from him extremes of feeling without ever knowing how or why. She recalled how one second he could freeze her with a dark frown and the next warm her with a tender look. And just when they were beginning to get acquainted, he'd walked out of her life as casually as he'd walked in.

With a noncommittal nod, Kara acknowledged his presence.

Bric bit back an oath. The sight of Kara hit him like a blow from a hammer. Seeing her again brought back all the simmering desire he thought he'd finally damped down.

Damn Carlisle! His partner just *had* to get the flu and stick him with the task of delivering these wedding guests!

His gaze ran over Kara's length, not missing the shock of surprise in her eyes. She looked wonderful. A fitted black coat outlined her slim waist and willowy figure. He wondered what it would feel like to splay his hand over her newly flattened stomach. Sliding his eyes back to hers, he returned her greeting with an abrupt slant of his head.

Kara turned to take Lynn from the car seat, then waited impatiently for the Parkers to join them on the church steps. A large woman, Mrs. Parker was having difficulty scooting out of the car, even with her husband's hands towing on one arm. It didn't help that Joey insisted upon running over to see Bric. Or that Bric gave the boy a cheery hello and ruffled the knit cap that covered Joey's head.

When the six-year-old skipped back to her, Kara took his hand and studiously avoided looking in Bric's direction. She couldn't prevent herself, however, from watching out of the corner of her eye as he assisted several elderly women from the van. His customary leather jacket was partly unbuttoned, revealing a tan shirt and striped tie. He wore creased slacks and polished loafers, and Kara found herself wondering if he still smelled of tangy after-shave mingled with the scent of the outdoors.

She breathed an almost audible sigh of relief that Bric was still occupied with his passengers when her own party began to climb the steps into the clapboard church.

The brief, traditional ceremony was followed by a noisy reception at Perry's only inn, a rambling nineteenth-century house that did a passable business during the warm months, when fishermen sought bass and perch in the lake waters and tourists visited the winery or relaxed on the picturesque beaches. The rest of the year, the inn served as a community center.

Carrying Lynn in her car seat, Kara walked into the dimly lit dining room. Wine and beer were already flowing freely. The wedding was providing the islanders with an unwonted winter celebration, and everyone seemed determined to make the most of the opportunity. Kara insisted that the Parkers mingle with their friends, assuring them that for Lynn's sake she'd rather sit at a corner table, as far away as possible from the disk jockey's speakers. She even volunteered to keep an eye on Joey, who was immediately drawn to the array of enticing food at the buffet table.

From across the room, Bric watched Kara settle the baby more comfortably in her carrier. Was she aware of how alluring she looked with her rich auburn hair piled in that loose swirl atop her head? His fingers ached to cup her slender neck and brush errant curls off her cheeks. In the past weeks he'd driven himself crazy thinking about her, but he'd steadfastly refused to go see her. He wouldn't be doing either of them any good to start something that could only end in heartache.

Music and the clink of glasses provided a lively background for the animated chatter surrounding him, but Bric was hardly aware of the noise. Longing to reacquaint himself with the feel of Kara in his arms, he sat in the shadows of the room and tried to be content with just looking. With easygoing grace she spoke to guests passing her table, got up to hug the young bride and groom, ushered Joey to the buffet and entertained Lynn. He shouldn't talk to her, but he knew it was only a matter of time before he would.

Kara lowered Lynn's car bed to the floor and tucked the blanket beneath her chin. "Such a good baby," she said, smoothing back a ringlet from the downy forehead. Smiling at Lynn's puckered response, Kara was suddenly aware that someone had come up behind her. As she got to her feet, a hand touched her shoulder.

"Mind if I take a peek?"

Even before she heard the deep voice she'd known the hand belonged to Bric. Kara drew away, more to escape his disturbing nearness than to give him a view of Lynn. He'd exchanged his leather jacket for a brown tweed sport coat. It was the first time Kara had seen him dressed in anything but jeans and a work shirt. He looked heart-stoppingly handsome.

"You're entitled," she replied evenly.

Bric lowered himself to a knee and pulled back the blanket. "She's grown," he observed, enchanted by the rosy-cheeked face and sturdy little body. Could a baby get that big in a little more than a month?

"Of course she has. She's six weeks old today."

Bric didn't fail to catch the hint of censure in Kara's remark. He lifted a tiny hand, which closed over his finger with a strength that both startled and pleased him. For a long second he let himself enjoy the sensation. Reluctantly he slipped from Lynn's grasp and replaced her blanket. Glancing a fingertip over the dimple in her chin, he whispered, "You're living up to your name, little one. You're lovely."

When Bric straightened, he turned to find Kara seated at the table. "I'm sorry not to have looked in on you these past weeks, but the ice fishermen have kept me pretty tied up." He claimed the chair next to hers. "At least I left you in good hands. How long were your parents here?"

"They could only stay a week." While her eyes searched his, her fingers blindly pleated the corners of a paper napkin. "You don't have to apologize, Bric. You don't owe us. Actually, we owe you." At his questioning look, she elaborated. "For three flights. The shopping trip and to and from the hospital. You never did bill me."

"On the house."

"But I can't—"

"No arguments. It's my gift. If you won't accept it for yourself, consider it a present to Lynn."

Before she could lodge another protest, Ruth tapped her on the arm. "Can I give Lynn her bottle?"

Relieved at the intrusion, Kara circled the girl's waist and pulled her close. "Of course you can. When she cries, we'll get it warmed in the kitchen." She gave the twisted waist of the little girl's smocked dress a gentle tug and hugged her tighter.

"Can I watch her till then?"

Kara smiled. "That would be a big help."

"No, if Ruth gets to feed her, I get to watch!" Joey protested. The boy had wandered over from the buffet, juggling a glass of punch in one hand and three chocolate cookies in the other.

"Both of you can keep an eye on her," Kara said to appease them. "Joey, why don't you tell me when she wakes up. I might have trouble hearing her cry over the noise."

Bric chuckled. "Noise is right. That music's as loud as it is disjointed! Matter of fact, this song is the first decent one I've heard all afternoon. Why don't we take advantage of these two eager sitters and dance?"

Before Kara could answer, he shoved back his chair, held out a hand and drew her up. Disarmed, she permitted him to link his fingers with hers and guide her across the room.

On the small, crowded floor, Bric enfolded Kara in his arms. Both hands pressed against her back, he fitted her soft curves to the hard planes of his body. As he and Kara began to sway to the slow tempo of a love song, his cheek came to rest against her temple.

Helplessly she settled into the warm embrace, her slender arms circling his neck. How different it felt from dancing with Edmund, who had always held her with one hand at her back, the other curved at her side, and who had invariably kept a respectable inch between them. Though Edmund had a superb sense of timing and led her effortlessly, whether they moved to a waltz or a tango, dancing with Bric was far more sensuous, far more pleasurable.

Perhaps, Kara reproached herself, she shouldn't enjoy it so much, this intimate brush of thigh against thigh. Nevertheless, she hesitated only a split second before laying her cheek against Bric's chest and leaning into his solid strength.

Bric wondered if she could hear the rapid pounding of his heart. How many times had he imagined holding her like this? But he hadn't dreamed it would feel so good, so right. Now, how was he going to back off before they were both sorry? How, when he wanted nothing more than to maneuver her into a dark corner where he could explore her mouth and stroke her body until the two of them were weak and senseless?

Bric closed his eyes and allowed his imagination free rein. He knew exactly how he would kiss her. He'd begin softly, gently, savoring each touch, each flavor of her. Feathering kisses over her face, down her throat, he'd keep her sweet lips till last. Until neither of them could bear the deprivation a moment longer. With the tip of his tongue he'd trace the fullness of her mouth, flicking across its center, teasing it to open to him.

A shudder trembled through him as he pictured the kiss deepening, growing hungrier. Without realizing it, Bric began to slide his hands protectively up and down Kara's back while in his fantasy he sipped and learned the secret recesses of her mouth. A hot shaft of desire sped through him, and he felt an answering hardness in his loins. He realized then that he'd know no peace until he'd made love to her. He also suspected he'd know no peace once he did.

Kara drank in the maleness of him. At every point where her body met his, she felt a throbbing pulse as though each pore were alive and wanting. His lips moved in her hair. One hand strummed up and down her back; the other pressed her head closer. With the stir of his body against her, it took all her willpower not to cushion him even further in her softness.

The choice was taken from her as he pressed his hands against her rounded bottom and urged her nearer to assuage his aching need. Her mind told her she ought to resist, to pull away; instead, she went weightless. Her legs seemed to be made of rubber, and she was certain they'd give way if Bric's arms weren't supporting her.

"I've dreamed of holding you like this," he murmured into her ear. "I don't know if I'll be able to let you go when the music stops."

"I'm not sure I'll make it back to the table if you do," she confessed, her mind too clouded to dissemble.

Against her cheek she felt his chest vibrate with silent laughter. "You're not alone."

Shaken, Kara looked up into his eyes. They appeared almost black in the shadowy room. "Maybe we'd better sit down."

"Give me a minute." He put a little space between them and struggled for control. "Ever been snowmobiling?" he asked out of the blue.

Her light laughter masked a nervous uncertainty. "You're full of surprises!"

"Is that so?"

"Yes, it is. I haven't quite figured you out."

"Good. That'll give you something to do while we go snowmobiling."

The music stopped to a burst of applause. As they wound their way back to Kara's table, she objected, "You assume a lot, John Brickner."

He pulled out her chair. "You can't live on the lake and not experience the thrill of speeding over the ice. It's good and thick this year. Plenty safe. Next Saturday all right?"

Even though Kara knew she was being railroaded, she was tempted. How long had it been since she'd done anything carefree and a little crazy? So long that she couldn't even remember. Had she ever? But if she'd once been free, she wasn't now. She had Lynn to think of.

Nor could she dismiss that sizzling dance. She could still feel the fiery imprint of his masculine form all the way from her thighs to her breasts. No, she wasn't sure it was wise to see Bric again. If she could believe the evidence of his body, he desired her. And in one sense she was grateful. At least she hadn't imagined an attraction that never existed. But how long could it last? How could she ever trust a man who ran hot and cold?

Kara glanced over at Lynn, flanked by her two small guards. "You forget I have a baby. I can't go running off and leave her."

"No, you can't." With a knuckle he lightly traced the line of her cheekbone. "But won't Mrs. McCann sit for you?"

"I suppose I could—"

"Then it's a date. I'll be by about one-thirty." Bric didn't give her a chance to come up with another excuse. He drew a pad and pencil from his shirt pocket and scribbled a hurried list. "This is what you'll need. If you don't have the outfit, I'm sure you can borrow one from somebody on the island."

A small smile of anticipation curved her mouth. "It would be fun. I guess I should take up some winter sports. And I'd love to see the island covered with snow."

Bric heard his name being called and looked up to see Mr. Linskey flagging him from the other side of the room. "I wish I could stay longer, but I'm being paged." He sent the groom's father a brisk nod. "I expect my passengers are ready to go.'' His fingers trailed down her arm before he left the table.

Kara followed his fluid gait as he answered Wayne Linskey's summons and rounded up his passengers. Why had she reacted so strongly and so immediately to Bric's powerful arms and the heated thrust of his body against hers? It was unlike her to behave as shamelessly as she had on the dance floor. What was she trying to prove, anyway? Had Edmund left her feeling so inadequate as a woman that she went overboard at the first touch of another man? What really frightened her was that Bric might expect more than she was prepared to give. Agitated, Kara ran a hand over her hair. What had she gotten herself into?

Lynn picked that moment to set up a fuss, which quickly diverted her mother's attention. As Bric left the dining room, he smiled at the sight of Kara lifting the baby into her arms. The little girl had a good set of lungs for such a tiny package, he mused. Determined, like her mother. It appealed to him, the combination of backbone and fragility. And passion. Strong passion. He had proof now that it lurked just beneath the surface of Kara's polished beauty. If only he'd known her years ago. Bric heaved a sigh. That was fate for you.

Outside dusk was falling. Chauffeuring the mainlanders back to the airport, Bric viewed the overcast sky with a sense of foreboding. Whatever the consequences, he'd committed himself. He only hoped Kara would understand that he wasn't all that she needed. For as long as it lasted, he would give her what he could and pray it would somehow be enough.

For both of them.

Chapter Five

For the sixth time, Kara went to her living-room window and peered out onto the frozen landscape. "I never should have agreed to this," she muttered under her breath.

Cradling Lynn in her arms, Delia McCann Linskey unconsciously matched her movements to those of her teacher. "Why don't you sit down, Mrs. Reynolds? As Mom says, a watched pot never boils. Anyhow, that rug's in none too good a shape, and the school board's not about to buy a new one. All you'll have to cover your floor is this old thing with a hole in it." As if to set a good example, she lowered herself and Lynn onto the rocker.

Kara rolled her lips together, struggling to hold back a laugh. What must Delia think of her! A grown woman behaving like a flustered teenager waiting for her first date. With as much dignity as she could summon, she settled onto a chair. But she couldn't stay put for long. Before she knew it, she was back at the window.

"What's keeping him?" Kara mumbled, clicking her pink nails nervously on the sill. It had been years since she'd had anything remotely resembling a date, and she wasn't sure whether to be worried by Bric's tardiness or merely annoyed.

"He'll be here," her student affirmed serenely. With one foot she tapped the floor and set the rocker in motion.

Amused by the contrast between the younger woman's newfound maturity and her own childish behavior, Kara turned away from the window. "I appreciate your offer to take care of Lynn for a couple of hours, but I sort of expected your mother. After all, you and Sam should still be on your honeymoon."

"I'm more than happy to do it, Mrs. Reynolds. It'll give me some practice." Instantly her face reddened. "Oh, I didn't mean to say that," she stammered, bringing the rocker to a sudden standstill.

Kara walked over to sit on the wide arm of Delia's chair. Of all her students, this one was in many ways the most sensitive. And perhaps the brightest. "Don't worry, dear. I already knew. It wasn't difficult for a recently pregnant lady to recognize the signs."

"I'm sure everybody suspects," the young woman added dismally. "It's not that I'm ashamed. I love Sam, and I don't care who knows it." Her chin slanted upward at a proud angle. "Still," she continued, "the way I was brought up, it's hard—" Delia broke off and looked directly at her teacher, her blue eyes pleading for reassurance.

"I understand," Kara commiserated. Being the object of neighbors' covert speculation was bound to hurt. Hadn't she herself once been the victim of wagging tongues? "For what it's worth, I want you to know that I respect your decision. After all, you could have flown over to the mainland to a private clinic. No one would have been the wiser."

"I couldn't have done a thing like that," Delia insisted, horror coloring her tone. "Not even if Sam had run off and left me. Of course—" she grinned mischievously "—on this island he couldn't have gotten very far, could he?"

The two women shared a laugh before Delia again grew serious. "Really, I don't see how any woman could give up her baby."

"I know what you mean." Kara studied the earnest face of her star pupil. When Kara had first come to Perry's last fall, she'd hoped to interest Delia in furthering her education, but it had soon become apparent she would be fighting a losing battle. Nevertheless, Kara regretted having never broached the subject.

Gently probing, she remarked, "Some women who get pregnant feel they aren't ready for motherhood, especially if they're looking forward to a career."

Delia vigorously shook her head. "That's not for me." As she smiled down at Lynn, her expression grew wistful. "You see, I've loved Sam ever since we were in first grade and he spent every recess chasing me around the school yard. All I ever wanted was to marry him and have a family. When I found out about the baby, well, I was scared. But Sam was so sweet. He went with me to tell my folks. It was sure a relief when they took it so well. Though it was kind of embarrassing having to move up our wedding date. People look at me funny sometimes."

Kara rubbed a comforting hand over Delia's shoulder. "Maybe you're only imagining that. The important thing is you feel you've made the right decision, one your families support. They're the ones who matter. So don't worry about what others may think."

Delia's eyes brightened. "I hadn't thought about it like that."

"Well, then, it's time you did."

"You're so nice to talk to, Mrs. Reynolds. You always know the right thing to say. And do."

"That's high praise indeed, and more than I deserve." Kara's gaze fell to her lap. "Believe me, Delia, I've made my share of mistakes."

"I can't believe that. You do everything so well. And all on your own, too." The young woman's face was full of admiration.

"Not quite," Kara insisted as her arm slid around Delia's shoulders. "I couldn't manage without help from some wonderful people like you and your mother. I'm glad you're both my friends."

The compliment brought a shy flush of pleasure to Delia's cheeks. "I guess we women have to stick together."

"I'll vote for that. Now," Kara said airily, "how about a cup of tea?"

"That would be nice." Delia resumed her rhythmic rocking of Lynn. "Do you have any without caffeine?"

"Does a blend of herbs, fruits and berries sound good?" When Delia nodded, Kara went to the kitchen and put on the kettle. Just as it began to boil, she heard the low rumble of an engine in the distance. Her heart surged with relief.

When a knock sounded on the door, Delia asked, "Should I let him in?"

"No, I'll do it." With studied indifference, Kara measured the loose tea into a pot. If John Brickner thought she'd rush to welcome him with open arms when he was nearly an hour late, well, he could just stand outside and cool his heels until she was good and ready to open the door!

After taking her own sweet time to ease from behind the counter, she crossed the room, then with a firm twist on the knob swung the door open. The action seemed to snatch her breath away. But Kara wasn't certain whether it was the sudden blast of bone-chilling wind or the bone-melting sight of Bric that had the air rushing from her lungs.

Outfitted in a two-piece insulated suit that boldly emphasized his masculinity, he stood with his weight on one foot and greeted her with a captivating grin. "Sorry I'm late."

Kara checked her watch. "Only fifty minutes or so," she observed evenly. She wasn't about to reveal that he'd in the least provoked her . . . or worried her.

To be honest, she'd been more concerned than irritated. And apparently with good cause, she thought. Her gaze traveled to the lethal-looking machine parked in her front yard. All that rubber and metal must pack quite a wallop. She wouldn't put it past the daredevil in John Brickner to rev it up well over a hundred miles an hour.

"Aren't you going to ask me in?" he inquired on a puff of cold air. "In case you hadn't noticed, you're losing a lot of heat."

Flustered, Kara moved aside, convinced there ought to be a law against a man looking that irresistibly male.

Bric stomped the snow from his boots before stepping over the threshold and pushing back his hood. "At the last minute I decided to check the engine one more time. We'll be going out on the lake, and I didn't want to risk getting stranded."

Kara smiled. She should have known as much. Bric might give the impression of being foolhardy, but he didn't take unnecessary chances. He might fly through a blinding snowstorm if the occasion warranted, but he was also the same man who had insisted upon repairing a door he considered unsafe. She found the combination of daring and discretion undeniably appealing.

Suddenly Kara's fingers itched to smooth down disturbed strands of Bric's thick dark hair. Shoving both hands into the pockets of her heavy wool pants, she offered, "I'm making some tea. Would you like a cup?"

"I'll pass, but I don't mind waiting while you have some. Serves me right for being late." With a knowing wink at Delia, Bric pulled off his gloves and partially unzipped his suit.

"Don't bother to take off your parka. Let me fix Delia's tea, and we can be on our way."

As she poured the boiling water into the pot, Kara watched Bric out of the corner of her eye. She felt a constriction in her chest when he walked over to hunch down for a closer look at Lynn. She wondered why he hadn't married and raised a family. It wasn't because he didn't like children. She remembered how good he'd been that day in the woods with Joey. And he always seemed so taken by Lynn.

Kara set the cup of tea on a table alongside the rocking chair before struggling into the down-filled jump suit she'd borrowed from Delia. After pulling on her boots, she bent to kiss Lynn. "We won't be too long," she whispered, more to assure the sitter than the sleeping infant.

"Don't you worry about a thing. We'll get along fine," Delia predicted. "Sam'll be over a little later to keep me company, so there's no need to hurry back. I figure the more time Sam spends with Lynn, the better prepared he's going to be."

The two women exchanged a secret smile.

"The refrigerator's pretty well stocked. You and Sam help yourself to anything you want." Kara gave the two slowly rocking figures a final farewell before slipping on her mittens and preceding Bric out the door.

Immediately a sharp wind bit into her face. Some new records for low temperatures had been set in the past few weeks. Today promised no break from the frigid air sweeping down from Canada.

Kara tucked her hood closer around her. Anyone venturing out in this cold had to be a little crazy. As another numbing gust hit her, she shuddered to think what it would feel like when that black-and-silver machine was cutting through the open air at who knew how many miles an hour!

Though she suspected she'd taken leave of her senses, Kara had to admit she was looking forward to the experience. She couldn't remember the last time she'd gone out simply to have a little fun.

Bric read uncertainty in the slight wrinkling of her brow. "Having second thoughts?" he asked, his breath a frosty ribbon on the wintry air. "Take my word for it. You're going to love riding on this beauty."

He slid a full-face helmet over Kara's head and tightened the strap beneath her chin. "To protect that flawless skin from the elements."

A tingle of pleasure rushed through Kara, warming her. After she'd taken her place on the seat behind him, Bric shouted above the noise of the engine, "Hold on."

Complying, Kara circled her arms around his body and locked her hands at his waist.

During the next hour they sped over nearly every square inch of Perry's Island, pausing occasionally for Bric to point out features of special interest. Not that such minute exploration was all that difficult, since, as he told her, the island took up no more than six square miles of Lake Erie.

When Kara had first arrived on Perry's, she'd tried to sort through the mess that was her life by seeking solace in its vineyards, woods and beaches. But once school had started, she hadn't had time for leisurely walks, especially in October, when the children of migrant grape pickers temporarily doubled the size of her class.

Although enchanted by the island in the waning days of summer, Kara wasn't prepared for its spectacular winter beauty. On this crystal-clear afternoon, the scenery reminded her of a glacial fairyland.

So captivating was the snow-covered landscape that Kara was barely alert when the snowmobile glided to a halt along Salter Woods, where her class had searched for a Christmas tree.

Bric switched off the engine and raised the visor of his helmet. "Like to stretch your legs?"

"You bet." Though the heavy outfit had kept her fairly warm, Kara was beginning to feel the cold seep into the tips of her fingers and toes.

Bric swung a leg over the front seat, stuffed his gloves into his helmet and slung the leather strap over a handlebar. Hanging Kara's headgear next to his, he held out a hand.

Even through fur-lined mittens, she felt his fingers curl around hers. She could no more control the immediate leap of her pulse than she could have swum across Lake Erie. With a casualness that belied her tension, Kara prudently withdrew her hand and tucked it in her jacket pocket. But her retreat proved futile when Bric draped an arm loosely around her shoulders.

The afternoon light faded as they entered the thick forest. Almost at once the temperature seemed to become moderate, with the trees and undergrowth providing a dense windbreak. Even so, a shiver of awareness trickled down Kara's spine as Bric drew her closer.

What the woman did to him! Bric marveled. Her scent, a heady mixture of wildflowers, reminded him of the soft breezes of spring. If it was spring, he'd lower her onto a feathery bed of ferns and learn every inch of her delicious body. Just thinking about Kara lying naked beneath him heated the blood racing through his veins.

Only the crunch of their boots over the snow-covered ground broke the enveloping quiet. Bric acknowledged that more than simple desire sparked his interest in this woman. Beneath her aura of fragility lay a steely strength that pulled at him irresistibly.

Bric surveyed her fine-boned profile. "Beautiful," he breathed into the cathedral-like stillness, hardly aware that the words had left his lips.

"Even lovelier than the last time we were here."

The January snows had worked their winter magic, blanketing the earth with a pristine purity. Like a picture on a Christmas card, the trees seemed frozen in a scene where nothing changed, nothing stirred.

Then out of nowhere a frightened rabbit materialized and scurried across their path, startling Kara. Jumping backward, she fell into a snow-mantled evergreen and came to an awkward sprawl on her backside. On a ripple of laughter, she reached for Bric's outstretched hand and had nearly gained her feet when the springy tree limbs shot upward, propelling her straight into his arms.

A bit dazed and breathless, Kara struggled for solid ground. Despite their heavy outer garments, she was acutely aware of the hardness of Bric's chest. Glistening snow crystals that clung to the fringe of her lashes lent a special sparkle to the moment. As she again lifted a hand to clear her blurred vision, Bric's arms came around her.

"You look like a sugared candy," he murmured, his eyes darkening with desire. "Good enough to eat."

Before Kara knew what was happening, his mouth lowered over hers and swallowed her astonished gasp.

She was surprised by the gentleness of his kiss. It weakened her, confused her. Slowly, sensuously, Bric sipped at the droplets of snow, lifting them from the corners of her mouth. His tongue traced the sloping curve of her lips, then flicked across their parted center. Giving herself up to the persuasiveness of his sweet assault, Kara let her eyes shut.

Something intense...need, longing...raced through Bric. He'd known that once he felt her soft mouth against his, kissing her would never be enough. He'd have to have more.

And then what? he asked himself.

Ruthlessly Bric thrust the nagging question aside. Where Kara Reynolds was concerned, he seemed to have no control.

Even cocooned in a bulky suit, her warm body and soft, feminine curves didn't escape him.

Kara's emotions were rocked by the tenderness of Bric's mouth. She felt as if she'd been buried under an avalanche. Every limb was burdened by a heaviness that made it impossible for her to move. She couldn't think. She couldn't see. She couldn't breathe.

She could only feel.

Bric's lips took a languid journey from one corner of her mouth to the other. Along the way, his tongue gently probed, seeking entry. For the barest fraction of a second, Kara thought to deny him. But she couldn't. No more than she could deny herself. Like ice in the sun, she melted into him.

Bric felt her body go pliant and moaned his pleasure. Despite the chilling cold, he was sorely tempted to make love to her then and there. Right on the snow-encrusted ground, with the wind softly stirring the tops of the pines. Crazy. Absolutely crazy. All the same he couldn't get enough of her. Her scent, her flavor, her taste.

The kiss was filled with warmth and promise. So much promise. Never, he thought, had any woman affected him so profoundly. Never had any sent his senses skating in ten different directions at the same time.

His fingers located the drawstring at her throat and loosened the knot. He pushed the hood back to free her hair. Smoothing away wispy strands, alive and willful in the crisp air, he eased her head to one side. His lips trailed along the delicate line of her jaw to worry an earlobe, then glided downward to plant nibbling kisses at the sensitive pulse point of her throat.

The flames that licked at Kara's insides threatened to consume her. Even in the icy cold, her body burned as if it were on fire. In no time Bric had her blazing with need. Quickly. Too quickly.

The realization brought her up short. She was walking on thin ice, and before it cracked, she'd better head for shore.

Bric felt Kara draw away, then push forcefully against his chest. With a painstaking lack of haste, he lifted his mouth and trapped her face between his hands. She looked so vulnerable, so wary...so stricken. Almost as if she'd seen the ghost of her husband.

On that desolate thought Bric stepped back. As jealousy welled within, his lips compressed into a hard line. It was an unfamiliar sensation for him, this bitter envy, and he was shocked by its intensity.

While the seconds spun out, Bric battled for emotional control. There were a thousand questions he wanted to put to her, but at the same time he didn't want to hear the answers. He didn't want to know how much she'd loved another man, even if he was dead. *Especially* if he was dead. When it came to those who were gone, the mind tended to remember the good and overlook the bad. What chance did he, a blemished male specimen, stand against the flawless memory of her husband?

"If we're going to make it home before dark, we'd better get moving," he finally managed to say around the tightness in his throat.

Minutes later Kara was straddling the snowmobile's broad leather seat and straining to catch the words Bric bellowed above the growl of the engine. She nodded when she finally made out that he was taking her for a short spin on the lake.

Before the powerful machine broke across the beach, Kara spotted fishing shanties scattered over the ice. Earlier Bric had told her that from the air they resembled clusters of small villages. Each evening they disappeared, only to re-form the following morning when ice guides led out parties of fishermen for a day of sport. The portable village ahead was already beginning to break up. Kara knew that the men had to be piloted to the mainland before dark, and the passenger plane could accommodate no more than nine or ten at a time. It must be later than she thought.

After they whizzed by the makeshift community, Bric immediately kicked up the speed. Kara had no idea how fast they were traveling, but tearing across the lonely, windswept desert of white gave her a glorious sense of freedom. Every bump on the frozen surface seemed magnified a thousandfold. Each time they hit an imperfection, she was amazed that she didn't go sailing straight through the air.

Gradually Kara allowed her body to snuggle into Bric's, her head to rest against his back. Worldly cares evaporated in the sheer thrill of the ride. Mellowed by a rare sense of euphoria, she closed her eyes.

Bric was bringing them out of a tight turn when a loud thwack punctured her reverie. The next instant the engine sputtered, coughed and died. For long seconds they glided noiselessly over the ice before coasting to a stop.

"What's wrong?" she asked.

"I'm not sure."

Swinging off the snowmobile, Bric squatted beside it. A few minutes passed while he poked and prodded the numerous tubes, valves and cylinders. All at once his eyes narrowed, and a torrent of pungent oaths blistered the frigid air.

"That serious, huh?"

With a sigh of exasperation, he admitted, "The drive belt broke and wrapped itself around the clutch."

"Which means? In simple English—"

"We're stuck." Bric couldn't help giving the broken-down machine an angry kick.

As Kara searched the boundless wintry expanse, an eerie feeling shivered along her skin. How far from home were they?

The telling nibble of her lower lip had Bric cursing his show of temper. "Come on," he said gently, offering a hand.

She crooked a leg and threw it over the large seat. "Where to?" So far as she could tell, they were miles from any sign of land, and it had to be a long way back to Perry's.

"Mahler's Island."

"Mahler's Island? I never heard of it."

"Not surprising. It's so small it's rarely shown on maps."

"If it's so small, what good will it do us? Are there people there, phones?"

In an attempt to dispel her fears, Bric pretended a bravado he didn't feel. "What is this, twenty questions?" At Kara's dubious glance, he reluctantly confessed, "Doubtful to the first. No, to the second. But native ice fishermen keep a small cabin there. It's usually well provisioned. But even if we don't find food, at least it'll provide a warm shelter.

Kara smiled weakly and thrust aside her anxiety, along with the unsettling thought of being marooned with Bric. "I suppose we haven't much choice," she remarked, wondering if it was her imagination or if the sky actually had begun to darken.

"You're right on that score."

Before they started out, Bric rummaged through the storage compartment for a flashlight and compass, then took time to get their bearings. By his calculations, the island lay due north and couldn't be much more than a couple miles away. In fact, he thought he could make out some treetops silhouetted against the early-evening sky.

Pointing across the lake, Bric directed Kara's gaze toward what he assumed was Mahler's. "See that dot on the horizon? That's where we're headed."

"Ready if you are," Kara claimed, striving for a reasonable facsimile of her normal voice.

It was hard going over the ice. As they slowly slipped and slid their way toward the tiny speck, seemingly making little progress, Kara began to feel swallowed up by the white world that encircled them. Finally she screwed up enough courage to ask, "What happens after we reach the cabin?"

Bric knew what he'd like to have happen, but he doubted her thoughts were running in the same direction. Taking refuge in humor, he teased, "What did you have in mind?"

"Be serious," she scolded. "How will we get home?"

Bric pulled her to him. "It's not as grim as it seems. The McCanns and Linskeys are sure to report us missing. I predict we'll be rescued by tomorrow afternoon at the latest."

"Oh."

"Does the thought of spending the night with me bother you?"

"Of course not," she returned a little too quickly.

"Good, because I have no intention of letting you compromise me."

"I'll keep that in mind." Kara couldn't stop the corners of her mouth from lifting, but the smile faded as she added, "To tell the truth, I'm more concerned about Lynn than anything. I've never been away from her before."

"Don't worry. Until someone finds us, you can be sure Delia and Sam will take good care of her." Bric shrugged. "Try to think of it as their dress rehearsal."

Her eyes snapped to his. "You know?"

"It wasn't the world's best-kept secret."

"Before you arrived this afternoon, Delia and I were talking. She was worried about what people think."

"Given the moral fabric of today's society, I find that refreshing."

"I agree. She and Sam are really nice kids, but...well...they are awfully young. Sometimes I... That is, as their teacher, I feel I failed them."

"How's that?"

"I can't help asking myself if anyone ever talked to them about alternatives."

"What kind of alternatives?" Bric clipped out.

Too absorbed in trying to stay upright, Kara failed to notice that his voice was as frosty as the surrounding air. "Like college."

"Are they college material?"

Kara laughed, recalling Sam's resistance to anything remotely academic. "They're both bright enough, but Sam lacks the motivation. Delia, however, is another story. She really likes school."

"You don't have to go to college to be educated," Bric argued.

"Agreed. And the baby certainly complicates things," she went on. "Even if I'd discussed college with Delia earlier, I doubt she'd have considered adoption or..." Kara fell silent, not willing to complete the thought.

Bric's eyes became remote. "Or what?" he asked in a flat voice.

"You know, terminate the pregnancy."

"Terminate? Why not call a spade a spade? You're talking abortion."

Kara paled at his sharp tone. "Not a pretty thought, but for some people it's a solution."

"That depends."

For long moments they trudged on without speaking. Only their labored breathing broke the silence. Kara couldn't help wondering why Bric seemed so touchy. At long last she ventured, "Did I say something wrong?"

Looking down into her anxious face, Bric could have kicked himself. Couldn't he have picked a better time to get on his soapbox? Yet whenever he recalled how Elaine had cheated him, invariably the hurt erupted as anger. Intellectually he could accept her decision. After all, she'd had no way of knowing what the future held for him. But emotionally...that was another story.

He stroked Kara's shoulder. "Don't mind me. I get grumpy when my toes go numb. As their teacher, you're bound to be concerned about Delia and Sam. But they were planning to get married after graduation anyway. I doubt you could have changed Delia's mind."

"Thanks for confirming my instincts," she told him. "I didn't like to think I'd shirked my duty. Since Dad's a professor, I sometimes put too much emphasis on higher education. Even when I know it's not for everybody."

For a moment Bric's face clouded over. Then he slid his arm firmly around Kara's waist. "You're doing a wonderful job at the island school, Kara. Now, quit trying to borrow trouble."

Trouble. The word brought Kara back to their very real predicament. They seemed no closer to that smudge on the horizon than they had been fifteen minutes ago. "Are you sure that's an island out there?"

He pulled her closer. "Positive. Hey, don't worry. Everything's going to work out fine. Why, we may even run into some fishermen who'll help us get back to Perry's."

Kara took heart, along with a deep, calming breath. She knew she could rely on Bric. Hadn't he already managed to get her out of one impossible situation, flying her safely to the hospital through that terrible storm?

"Trust me," he urged as if he'd just read her thoughts.

"Easier done than said," she assured him.

Bric's heart began to hammer. Did she mean that as a declaration of her faith in him, or had she merely twisted around the old adage? Afraid to ask, he commented, "One more thing."

"What's that?"

"Keep talking. It'll make the time go faster."

"Tell me it'll make my feet go faster, and you've got a deal."

Chapter Six

It was twilight before Bric and Kara finally reached the crude shelter on Mahler's Island.

"At last," Kara forced through chattering teeth as she collapsed against the closed door. Despite the energy she'd expended putting one foot in front of the other, the biting cold had finally crept through her layers of clothing. In no time it had made its way to fingers and toes before invading arms, legs and torso. Added to that, she'd had trouble maintaining her balance on the ice. With every step her well-worn boots had threatened to skate out from under her. If it hadn't been for Bric, she would have fallen more than once.

"Let's see what we have here," Bric suggested, flipping on the flashlight and training its beam over the dim interior. A small cast-iron stove occupied the center of the room, while a scuffed cabinet leaned against one wall, a wooden table and two straight-back chairs against another. In the far corner was a rudely constructed bunk.

"Seems the old rule still holds," Bric remarked.

"What old rule?"

"If you use the shelter, you're supposed to leave it ready for the next visitors." He sniffed. "Smells a little musty from being shut up but seems neat and clean enough. Including that bed. Sure looks inviting, doesn't it?"

"I can't argue with that." Now that they were no longer battling the elements, Kara's taut body registered the strain of the past ninety minutes. Try as she might, she couldn't keep her shoulders from sagging into a telltale droop.

In one fluid motion, Bric swept her into his arms. "Don't get the wrong idea," he advised as he carried her toward the bunk and carefully lowered her onto the covers, "but you look beat. Why don't you try to catch a few winks while I check things out?"

Gratefully Kara let her body sink into the quilted comforter. "Don't mind if I do," she got out only seconds before her eyes closed.

Bric's search turned up candles and matches, towels and bedding, pots and pans, an assortment of dishes, some extra-heavy wool blankets and an ample supply of coffee, tea, powdered eggs, milk and soups.

After lighting the candles and placing them around the room, Bric shook out one of the blankets and covered Kara, who still looked cold despite her heavy outer garments.

"Now to get a fire going," he announced to the bare walls. Picking up the ax he'd found propped beside the door, Bric walked back outside. Just as he'd suspected, a cord of wood was stashed behind the cabin. Before long he'd split enough kindling to have the small stove crackling with warmth.

Once the chill was out of the air, he shucked off his cumbersome snowmobile suit, melted some icicles in a kettle and finally turned back to Kara. After loosening her hood and drawing off her mittens, Bric rubbed both slender hands in his. "Getting thawed out?" he asked as her eyes opened.

"I think so. It feels like a mad acupuncturist has jabbed a million needles in my toes."

"A sure sign Jack Frost didn't nip them off." As she shimmied up against the headboard, he went on, "If you can stand the cold, you'll find some primitive facilities out back. Sorry the accommodations aren't more plush." Bric returned to the stove and added more wood to the fire.

"I hadn't noticed," she confessed, rolling to her feet. "That's a surprisingly comfortable bed."

"Big enough for two?"

At his grin, Kara's heart set up an erratic flutter. Did he plan for them to sleep together tonight? "Sorry," she said with a forced flippancy, "but I'm claiming squatter's rights."

"Don't be greedy. You wouldn't want me to freeze to death, would you?"

"With your back to that roaring fire?"

"Heartless woman! You expect me to stand here all night? What if we run out of wood?"

"I have it on good authority that you're quite resourceful when it comes to chopping down trees." Her voice came out a bit unsteady, and she nervously cleared her throat. "I think I'll avail myself of the outdoor amenities."

"When you come back, do you want coffee or tea?"

"I have a choice?"

"That's only for starters. The main course is cream of chicken soup."

"You're not pulling my leg, are you?"

"Hmm, a tempting thought, but no." At her blush, one corner of his mouth tipped up. "For your information, right now I consider food too serious to be a joking matter. Now, hurry up, or you'll be late for supper."

Kara made it a fast trip. When she returned to the cabin, she removed her jump suit and accepted a cup of coffee from Bric. While she sipped the hot brew, she assessed the supply of food. Enough for at least a week. Somehow that knowledge was both comforting and unsettling.

Not that the place wasn't adequate, she admitted as she sat down on a rickety chair. Even the chilly outhouse had been tolerable. But what if they were stuck here for days?

To begin with, she didn't like to think about being separated from Lynn that long, even if her daughter was in good hands. Equally unnerving was the thought of being isolated with Bric. Kara frowned as she swallowed the last of her coffee.

"Something bothering you?" Bric probed, setting a mug of soup in front of her.

"I keep wondering when we'll be found."

"Believe me, it won't be long. Besides the McCanns and Linskeys, you can count on my partner to report us. When I fail to check in tonight, he'll have the whole coastal service mobilized at dawn."

After they'd finished their meager meal, Bric leaned back and rolled up his shirtsleeves. "It's getting warm in here. Don't you want to shed some of those clothes?"

"Good idea." Kara started to unzipper her cross-country pants. To her dismay, the slide became snagged in the nylon. She got to her feet and alternately coaxed and tugged at the slippery fabric, but her efforts were useless.

"Blast," she muttered, "it's stuck but good."

Bric rounded the table. "Let me try. Maybe I can get it from a different angle." His hands replacing hers, he eased the tab up and down several times and eventually managed to free the material.

"You're a genius," she proclaimed. "A few more minutes and I'd've ripped it." Her grateful gaze lifted to meet his.

Time melted away as their eyes locked and held. Then Bric slipped his fingers beneath Kara's waistband. When he slowly began to lower the nylon over her hips, she felt herself flush with a warmth that had nothing to do with the temperature of the room.

"I can do that," she objected. Backing away, she skimmed the pants down legs grown suddenly wobbly. But when she sat down and attempted to pull them over her heavy chukkas, she again met with defeat.

Flashing an amused grin, Bric hunkered before her. "That won't work," he asserted as he took over and loosened the boot laces.

First one boot and then the other plunked to the floor. Before Kara could protest, the cross-country pants quickly followed. Though his hands were more efficient than intimate, Kara was extremely conscious of Bric's touch. Nevertheless, it beat the embarrassment of having to undress herself while he watched.

Bric got down to leg warmers and two pairs of socks before he uncovered wool slacks over her footed tights. His mouth quirked in a droll smile. "You sure climbed into a lot of clothes. You weren't expecting to get lost on a forsaken island, were you?"

She scrunched up her face. "Delia told me to wear as much as I could without cutting off my circulation."

"I'd say you took her advice to heart. Let's see what all you managed to stuff on top."

"Patience," Kara returned. Feeling more in control, she rose to remove the suede vest and bulky sweater that concealed her pale blue turtleneck.

Bric was having trouble reining in his wayward imagination. So often during the past week his mind had replayed their sensuous dance at the wedding, and he wanted more than anything to take Kara in his arms again. Their kiss in Salter Woods had only fueled his desire. But he knew their exhausting day had left her defenseless, and he had no intention of taking advantage of the situation.

Still, while she folded her clothes and laid them in a neat bundle, he couldn't prevent his eyes from wandering over the knit fabric that plainly outlined the upward thrust of her breasts.

Before his mind's eye could strip Kara right down to her velvety skin, he grabbed the kettle from atop the stove. "I'm going to do the dishes," he declared gruffly.

The abrupt shift in Bric's mood puzzled Kara. One minute he'd been laughing good-humoredly; the next he seemed annoyed. Maybe he was irked because she'd tumbled into a weary heap when they'd arrived at the cabin. It seemed that most of the time they were together, Bric was taking care of her one way or another. He'd probably had his fill.

Instead of moving toward the stove, Kara walked over to the cabinet where he was pouring hot water into an enameled pan. Laying a hand on his arm, she nudged him aside. "Let me wash these. I'm beginning to feel like a charity case."

Lost in his own emotional struggle, Bric jerked around the instant her fingers met the sleeve of his wool shirt. "What do you mean, a charity case?"

Shrugging, she picked up a mug and dipped it into the water. "You're always doing something for me. Fixing a door, taking me shopping, rushing me to the hospital. And today you got the fire going, fixed the coffee, heated the soup. And what have I done? Zilch, zero, nothing."

Bric shook his head. He could name more than a few things Kara had done for him, but he doubted she was ready to hear about them. He folded his arms across his chest and rested a hip on the counter. "I wasn't aware we were keeping score. But if you want to get technical about it, aren't you forgetting who got us into this jam in the first place?"

"Don't be silly, Bric. It wasn't your fault the drive belt broke."

"True, but I should have checked it out more carefully before we left. Obviously I missed something." He scoured a hand over the evening stubble that shadowed his face. "Hell, Kara, you have no cause to feel bad. I'm the one who got us stranded and wore

you out. Luckily Mahler's was close by, or we could
have frozen to death out there. If anybody should be
on a guilt trip, it's me. Not you.''

Kara's hand stilled in the water. As far as her feelings of guilt went, he'd seen only the tip of the ice-
berg. She wanted to argue that she had good reason to
be hard on herself. She wanted to tell him the truth
about Edmund and her marriage, to share the unhappy secrets she kept locked in her heart, but when
she looked up and opened her mouth to speak, he
placed a finger over her lips.

''Shh. I don't know what brought on that burst of
self-reproach. Aren't you the woman who refused to
run home to her parents and let them take care of her
and her baby? The one who accepted a job most
teachers would never even consider? The one who insisted on chopping down a Christmas tree when she
was eight-months pregnant? I don't want to hear any
more talk about charity cases. As a matter of fact, I
can't think of anybody I'd rather be stranded on an
island with.''

Kara wiped her hands along the sides of her slacks.
''If you're trying to win me over with flattery, I think
you ought to know it's working.''

At the look of pleasure in her eyes, Bric took a step
forward. His hands went to her waist and tugged her
close. ''Better not to think,'' he advised in a low voice.

As he tipped her face up, a quiver of excitement
trembled through Kara. For endless minutes he looked

into her eyes. Mesmerized, she watched the slow descent of his head.

As soon as their lips fused, something intense flared between them. Immediately Kara opened to him, and his tongue swept her mouth with a thoroughness that left her light-headed and giddy. Fearing her legs would give way, she skimmed her hands up Bric's back and clung to his shoulders for support.

His ravenous mouth left hers only to trail moist kisses over her temples, her eyes, her cheeks, forcing her attention to each sensitive point he explored.

"So soft, so tempting," he murmured hoarsely.

Her senses fogged, Kara sagged forward and pressed her cheek to his throat. Bric's warm breath fanned her face. The rapid thunk of his heart pounded in her ear. The sharp, masculine scent of him touched her nostrils. Without thinking, she slid her palms to his chest and worked open three buttons. Her eager fingers burrowed beneath his shirt to explore the muscled expanse and tangle in a cover of wiry hair.

Bric groaned, his mouth again swooping down to claim her lips in a mind-shattering kiss that threatened to rob Kara of all reason. Air backed up in her throat, and she couldn't push her thoughts past the moment. Automatically she lifted her arms to circle his neck and draw him closer.

Bric grasped her hips and pressed her to him, letting her feel his need. As the kiss grew hungrier and more heated, a small voice urged Kara to pull back. She was playing with fire. But she couldn't call a halt.

Not just yet. Not when her body was shaky with desire. Not when it felt so good to be cradled against his hard strength.

Never had a man drawn so much from her so fast. His hands, his mouth were teaching her more about herself than she'd ever known before. Forgetting to be wary, she yielded to him and let the sensations build.

Moaning, Bric pulled away, leaving her feeling suddenly bereft. "Oh, Kara. How I want you. I've wanted you a long time."

"I know," she answered softly, and nestled her head beneath his chin.

"You feel the same way, don't you?" His hands roamed the hollows of her back. "Don't you?" he repeated.

A tremor rocked through her. "Yes." The word was a bare whisper. "But—"

His mouth covered hers, swallowing her protest. With exquisite slowness he massaged first one breast, then the other, brushing his thumb back and forth across her sensitized nipples until they puckered with sweet pain. Gasping, Kara felt the delicious shimmer all the way to the tips of her toes.

When at last she and Bric drew apart, they were both breathing raggedly. Bric pressed his forehead to hers. "You feel wonderful, taste wonderful." As his mouth made new demands, his fingers began tugging the shirt from her slacks.

The cool air that whispered against her bare skin jerked her back to reality. Kara shivered. What was she doing? Had Edmund left her so sex-starved that at the first opportunity she was ready to fall into bed with a man? After only a kiss or two? And on their very first date?

Though it took every ounce of her strength, she brought her hands to his chest and pushed. "Bric, I can't."

"What's the matter?" he asked, his senses dazed.

"It's too soon."

"Too soon?" Releasing her, Bric ran a hand through his hair and struggled to bring his breathing back under control. No sooner had the full import of her words soaked in than he cursed himself for a heel. Of course it was too soon. Shaking his head, he conceded, "I don't know what to say. Forgive me, sweetheart. I should have realized. You're hardly back to normal after Lynn's birth."

The endearment sent a flush of pleasure to her cheeks, adding to her mortification. "I didn't mean... It isn't that I can't... That is, it is over six weeks. But, well, I've only been with one man. And it's—" her voice dropped to a whisper "—I'm simply not ready for this."

Bric's arms fell to his sides. She was still grieving for her husband. Hadn't he been reminded of that scant hours ago? And here he was steamrolling her again. Would he never learn? Both chagrined at himself and hurt to think that another man had greater title to her love, he slumped against the cabinet.

The expression that darkened Bric's features surprised Kara. She hadn't meant to be a tease. She should have guessed he'd be used to women who were a lot more sophisticated. Well, she'd gone this far. She might as well get it all out in the open and confess to what else was bothering her.

"There's another reason, too. I'm . . . you know . . . not prepared." She looked away, unable to meet his eyes. "Some liberated woman, huh?"

Bric opened his mouth, but no sound passed his lips. It was an argument he hadn't anticipated. And for good reason. He felt a sharp prick of conscience. Kara was being totally open with him. Shouldn't he return the favor? Even at the risk of scaring her off?

Kara joked lamely, "But then I don't suppose you're prepared, either."

A dry laugh rumbled up from Bric's chest. She couldn't have handed him a more perfect opportunity, and though it hurt like the devil, he might as well take the plunge and get it over with. Sooner or later she'd have to know.

His tone was raw with cynicism as he explained, "I'm afraid that's one item they don't stock around here. But it's not a problem, anyway. Because you see, Kara, I'm sterile."

The blunt announcement left her momentarily speechless. It was the last thing in the world she'd expected him to say, and she was uncertain how to respond. All she could do was stare, openmouthed.

If the situation was reversed, she could imagine how empty, how incomplete as a woman she'd feel. Could men feel just as deprived? Kara had only to look into Bric's face for an answer.

She extended both hands and held his jaw. "Do you want to talk about it?"

"I just did," he answered shortly. Though Bric searched her eyes for signs of pity and rejection, he found only sympathy and concern. At first relieved, then touched, he gathered Kara close. "Just let me hold you awhile."

His mind strayed to that other time he'd talked about his condition. Since Vietnam, Bric had been seriously involved with only one woman. Gloria. Blond, petite, pretty as a picture and, as it turned out, with about as much depth.

After things had begun to heat up between them and it appeared they might be headed for the altar, Bric had thought it only decent to tell her about this "disability." He'd been totally unprepared for Gloria's reaction. With a speed that had left him reeling, she'd summarily written him out of her life. Though he couldn't fault her for wanting children, her cool dismissal had held a censure that ripped him apart. Gloria's few heartless words wrote the final chapter to a scenario Elaine had started.

Never had Bric felt so cold, so empty, so less a man.

But it was Kara in his arms now, Kara to whom he owed an explanation. "I'm sorry if that disappoints you," he said flatly.

Though a flood of conflicting emotions clamored for her attention, Kara shunted them aside. It was more important now to offer Bric what comfort she could. She knew how much he liked children, how important they were to him. But instead of bemoaning his condition, here he was worried about how disappointed *she* might be to discover he was sterile.

Kara rested her hands on his shoulders and took a moment to consider what she should say. Because she didn't want to hurt or offend him, she'd have to walk a fine line between honesty and understanding. Finally she ventured, "I'm sorry, too. Sorry for what can't be. And I'm not going to insult you by saying it doesn't matter. Both of us know it does."

At Kara's words Bric's eyes iced over, and he twisted away. How foolishly he'd misread her initial response! In her tactful way, she was letting him down easy. He knew all along that in the end she'd never want a man who couldn't give her babies. A sickeningly familiar despair gripped him, leaving an aching hollow inside.

Bric marched over to the stove and poked at the fire, cursing the rotten hand fate had dealt him. He'd thrown his cards on the table now, and he couldn't blame her for folding on him. What was it the nurse had said? That Kara was made for having babies. Trouble was, she made him want them, too. She made him yearn to build a life, a family. He'd never met a woman he wanted so much to have his children.

An uneasy silence stretched between them until the tension was almost palpable. Kara longed to reach out to Bric, but it was only too obvious that her attempt to console him had failed miserably, and the last thing she wanted to do now was unwittingly add to his pain. With a sinking heart, she turned and began to wash the dishes.

Leaning the poker against the stove, he said self-mockingly, "Look at it this way. With me you'd never have to worry about ending up with your reputation compromised."

Kara whirled. "What's that supposed to mean?"

Jamming his hands in his back pockets, he snapped, "You have to ask?"

He knew that he was being unreasonable, that he could hardly blame Kara for a quirk of fate, but did it have to make so much difference? Couldn't she accept him as he was? A few minutes ago she'd been worried about getting pregnant. But as soon as she'd learned there was no chance of that, she suddenly found him lacking. Granted, her rejection wasn't as brutal as Gloria's, but as far as he was concerned, it was just as final.

Kara wrapped her arms around her body. "I'd like to know why you're so angry."

"I expected something different from you, that's all. But you're exactly like Gloria."

"Gloria?" Kara asked, trying to ignore an unreasonable pang of jealousy.

"The only other woman I ever came close to—" Bric broke off. "She was put off by my sterility, too."

"Is that what you think? That I . . . Bric, I said no such thing!"

"For a teacher, you have a deplorably short memory. Unless there's something wrong with my hearing, I could swear you just told me it *does* matter."

"What?" Kara was dumbfounded. "You're jumping to the wrong conclusion. I was thinking about you, how much it matters to you, when I said that."

"How diplomatic. But why not come right out with it? Tell me I'm only half a man. It wouldn't be the first time I've heard it."

Sympathy for Bric's obvious misery was instantly transformed to amusement as the ludicrousness of his statement struck Kara. "After you had my knees buckling with a single kiss, I'd say that point's up for debate."

"What did you say?"

At the anguished look on Bric's face, Kara's mirth evaporated. *He really believes I was rejecting him,* she thought. Her voice grew soft, serious. "How can half a man make me feel so much a woman?"

Nothing she could have said would have affected him more deeply, but he was afraid to believe her. "Kara, you don't have to pretend with me."

"Who's pretending?" Unable to stop herself, she walked into his arms. "I meant every word. Oh, Bric, I know how much it hurts to have someone you love cruelly reject you. But there's something more, isn't there? Something you're not telling me."

He sighed heavily. "You're right." Folding Kara in his arms, Bric realized he wanted to talk about it now. All of it.

He guided her to the edge of the bed, and they sat side by side on the mattress.

"I've never told anyone this," Bric began. "It's a long story."

"I'm not going anywhere."

He lifted a skein of burnished hair and sifted it through his fingers. "There was this girl in high school. Elaine."

"I thought her name was Gloria."

"Different time, different girl. You want the whole story, don't you?" At Kara's nod, Bric continued. "Well, it begins with Elaine. A redheaded fireball in more ways than one. We'd been going together about six months when she told me she was on the Pill. It was obvious what she wanted, not that I put up any great resistance. Besides, I was crazy about her. Maybe Elaine was lying. I don't know. Anyway, she got pregnant the spring of our senior year. I did what I thought was the right thing and asked her to marry me.

"Looking back on it, I'm not sure I was really in love, but I honestly felt we could make a go of marriage. At any rate, I started to plan on how I could get a job and go to school nights. I had our future all worked out. And I was excited about being a father. I even started wondering what color hair the baby would have. It was a mind-blowing experience for an eighteen-year-old. Scary, too, I'll admit, but it gave me a real sense of power to think I could do that. Make a human being. I considered myself a real man. I was actually looking forward to that baby.

"But Elaine had other ideas. She was headed for college and a career in law, which left no room in her life for a husband, much less a child. One day she called to say I didn't have to worry anymore about lining up a job. She'd had an abortion."

Kara sandwiched Bric's large hand between her two smaller ones.

"I felt betrayed. And powerless. As though she'd destroyed a part of me. I'd had no say in her decision. No control over what she did."

Kara tenderly touched his cheek. "That would be difficult to cope with. Especially for a teenager. But, Bric, if you fathered a child, how can you be sterile?"

"That's not the end of the story. For all the wrong reasons, I chucked college and joined the marines. I guess it was my way of proving my manhood. Before I knew it, I was flying choppers in 'Nam. One day I was headed out to pick up some wounded when I developed engine trouble and went down. Either the Vietcong didn't see me or else they left me for dead, because when I came to, I was alone in the wreckage. With a hell of a pain in my head . . . and my groin.

"My guardian angel must have been working overtime, because somehow I survived. It took me close to two weeks to make it to a friendly village, and by then I was raging with fever and half-delirious. The villagers had almost no food and nothing in the way of medical supplies, but they did their best to get the fever under control. Fortunately, it wasn't long before a field medical team lifted me to Saigon. But the outcome was that I'll never be able to father another child.''

He bowed his head. ''Maybe if Elaine hadn't taken from me the one I might have had, I wouldn't have been so angry over my sterility. But she did, so the accident seemed like an especially dirty trick.''

''Whoever said life was fair?'' Kara said soothingly, reflecting on the irony of their situation. Although Bric's disclosure had strengthened the bond between them, it had also erected an almost insurmountable barrier. Knowing how she felt about children, would she be doing the right thing, Kara pondered, to encourage a deepening of their relationship? Yet to turn her back on him now was unthinkable.

Her eyes followed the fine line etched across Bric's cheekbone. How neatly the surgeon had repaired this facial wound. Could she perform an equal miracle and help Bric heal those fierce inner lacerations that had ripped at his very soul?

Or in the end would she simply open old wounds?

Chapter Seven

Much to Kara's dismay, Bric abruptly stilled her finger as it trailed over the scar on his cheek. Though he brought the back of her hand to his lips, the gesture seemed to be more farewell than invitation. While the seconds slipped by, the silence blanketed them like a heavy fog. Only the sputter of dying embers broke the unnatural stillness.

When at last Bric got off the bed to tend the fire, he casually remarked, "I don't know about you, but I could use some shut-eye. Which side of the bed do you want?"

Kara didn't know whether to be pleased that he'd asked her preference or disturbed that they'd have to share the bunk. "This one's fine," she told him.

"Done," he said, and extinguished the candles.

By tacit agreement, they stretched out fully clothed. Though each hugged an edge, the narrow mattress made it impossible for them not to touch. Eventually they gave up trying to avoid contact and dozed off back to back.

The following morning, Kara awakened to find herself curved spoon fashion into Bric's warmth, his arm flung over her waist. During the night, her pullover had crept up, and his hand had tunneled beneath the material to find the bare flesh of her rib cage. With his breath whispering into her hair, his fingertips resting beneath her breast, his body curved around hers, she felt a tingling at every point their skin made contact. Nerves drawn tight, she lay motionless, scarcely daring to breathe.

Kara knew the precise moment Bric awoke. His body suddenly went rigid. Then he jerked his arm away, almost as if his hand had been touching hot coals. With a sound that could have been a moan or a curse, he threw back the quilt and bounded out of bed. Mumbling something about the morning coffee, he started to bang around the kitchen area.

With an exaggerated yawn, Kara slowly rolled out of bed. "How's a body supposed to get any rest with all that racket?" she teased, keeping her voice steady despite the knot of tension in the pit of her stomach.

Bric pivoted, his mouth slanted in a crooked grin. *She's trying to lighten me up,* he thought, and immediately felt himself relax. "Don't give me any sass, woman. Up with you! On your way to the necessary, you can fill the kettle with snow."

"Yes, sir." Kara executed a sharp military salute before pulling on her boots and coat. "And what will you be doing while I'm playing Jane to your Tarzan?"

"Would you believe swinging from the trees to find more kindling?"

She pulled her face into an off-center moue.

"I thought not." He gave her a friendly swat. "Now, move. I'm a real savage until I've had my morning coffee."

For a time, they clung to playful banter like a life preserver. But as the morning wore on, they felt more and more keenly the strain of ignoring an accidental touch or a telling look. By the time they sat over a makeshift breakfast of watery eggs and stale coffee, they were once more sharing a vague unease.

Much to Kara's relief, the boisterous shouts of a search party finally punctured the tense atmosphere. Before she could push back her chair, Mark Carlisle and the Linskeys were pounding at the door.

Since then, Bric had seemed as cautious as Kara about picking up where they'd left off on Mahler's. Barely a week after their ordeal, he showed up late one afternoon with a delivery of textbooks. When he strode into the classroom, Kara couldn't stem a small ripple of joy, but she did her best not to let it show.

Bric gave her only a polite nod and lukewarm smile as he deposited the heavy carton beside some bookshelves. While taking his leave, he bombarded her with a string of inconsequential questions, none inviting more than a monosyllabic reply. Would she like him to pry open the box? Had she caught a cold from their trek over the ice? Did she need anything? How was school going? Was Lynn well?

The visit left Kara with a terrible sense of emptiness and despair.

For Kara, the rest of February dragged by, one dismal winter day slipping monotonously into the next. Almost daily the overcast sky covered the island with a fresh layer of snow. It didn't help that Bric was once again making himself scarce. Or that since his revelation she, too, had felt the need for some space.

One dreary Sunday afternoon late in the month, Kara sat at her dining table, preparing assignments. She had just finished compiling vocabulary lists when soft gurgling sounds drew her to the bedroom. Lynn was cooing at the crib mobile, her sturdy little legs kicking, her small hands waving at the figures revolving gently above her.

"You always wake up happy, don't you, sweetheart?" Kara leaned over and nuzzled her head in Lynn's warm belly, eliciting a squeal of pleasure. "Even when you're sopping wet."

As if she understood, Lynn wrinkled her brow and puckered her mouth in a way that never failed to remind Kara of Edmund. The memory triggered a pang of conscience. Lately she'd had more and more difficulty justifying her decision to keep Lynn to herself.

Adding to her emotional burden, of course, was her turmoil over Bric. No sooner had their relationship gotten off the ground than his confession sent it into a tailspin.

The problem was that Kara wanted more babies. Not simply for her own sake but for Lynn's. She didn't like the idea of her daughter growing up as she had— a "lonely only." But at the same time she realized she was wildly attracted to Bric, a man who could never father a child.

With an effort, Kara pushed the niggling thoughts from her mind and changed Lynn's diaper. When she shifted her onto a hip, she was treated to endearing little babbles. "Charmer," Kara praised, reminded of how her daughter seemed to be the center of attention wherever they went on Perry's. Even Kara's students fought over who would feed her or rock her or hand her a toy. "Sometimes I'm afraid you're going to get spoiled with all that oohing and aahing," Kara worried aloud, "but I guess no one ever gets too much love. Now, how about watching Mommy work?"

Setting Lynn in the next room, Kara heard a rap on her front door. When she opened it, her eyes rounded in surprise. "Bric!"

"Hi." Self-consciously he shifted his weight from one foot to the other.

Kara's heart was fairly tripping over itself. She drew in a deep, steadying breath before asking, "What brings you to Perry's?"

"Just thought I'd see how things were going." What Bric couldn't tell her was that for the past weeks he'd been at loose ends. Nor could he admit that on this depressingly gray Sunday, he hadn't been able to find any work to distract him. He only knew he missed her and needed to see her.

"Won't you come in? Can I get you anything to drink? Coffee? Tea?" she offered, then took his jacket.

"Coffee'd be fine."

Bric sat down on the sofa while Kara pretended to be absorbed in filling the pot with water, measuring the grounds and plugging in the cord. The two of them were shying away from each other like a couple of hermit crabs, he thought, scraping a hand over his face.

He gave himself a mental kick. He should have planned more carefully what to say before he arrived. Breaking through the wall of reserve that separated them was going to be tougher than he'd imagined.

A small whimper put an end to his thoughts. He walked over to take a closer look at Lynn. "I'd have hardly recognized her," he announced to Kara. "She's growing up."

"I know. Two and a half months old, and already she's an armful."

Bric trailed the pad of his thumb down a chubby cheek. "Looks like your daughter could teach you a lesson or two."

Puzzled, Kara gaped at his puffed-out cheeks before it dawned on her what he was talking about. "Humph. You and Mrs. McCann! She's forever trying to fatten me up."

"Don't get me wrong. You look terrific. But...you could do with a couple of pounds."

Ignoring the implied criticism, Kara latched on to the compliment. It was the first completely unguarded, purely personal statement Bric had made to her in nearly a month, and she couldn't deny how good it made her feel.

She didn't have an opportunity to bask in the praise before Lynn set up a racket. Kara loosened the safety strap on the infant seat and picked up the squirming child.

"Is something wrong?" Bric asked a bit anxiously.

"Nothing that lunch won't cure."

"Want me to hold her while you get it ready?"

Kara was about to say that his offer wasn't necessary, that like all mothers she'd developed a real talent for working one-handed, but a certain wistfulness in his eyes stopped her. Tilting her head, she smiled up at him. "Are you sure? She can be a real terror when she's hungry."

"I'll take my chances."

"Don't say I didn't warn you."

The instant Bric's outstretched arms closed around her, Lynn's wails went up three decibels. At his woeful look, Kara added, "I almost forgot. She's getting to the age where she doesn't take kindly to strangers. Particularly men. Good luck.''

While Bric slowly paced back and forth with the baby, Kara busied herself in the kitchen. Off and on she stole an amused glance toward the living room. She had to give Bric his due. Though at first he handled Lynn a bit uncertainly, he soon grew more bold, gently jiggling and patting and keeping up a determined flow of prattle. Before long her crying lessened and eventually tapered off into ragged hiccups.

Just as Kara came back into the room, Lynn reached for Bric's nose. ''A little more to hold on to than your mother's, huh?'' he observed wryly. ''Well, go ahead and pinch it. We men aren't delicate.''

Though innocent, the remark shook Kara to the core. Until that moment, she hadn't considered how deprived Lynn might be, living with a single parent. No wonder her baby often shied away from men. She had no father to acquaint her with the rougher texture of a man's skin, the deeper pitch of his voice.

A dull throb began to hammer at the back of Kara's neck. Seeing Lynn's tiny fingers play over Bric's face, hearing his laughing indulgence, had awakened a painful realization. Unless Kara came to grips with her residue of hostility toward Edmund, their daughter was never going to know a father's love. And that wasn't fair—neither to Lynn, who shouldn't have to pay for her parents' shortcomings, nor to Edmund, who, in spite of all he'd done to Kara, had a right to know his child.

As the pounding at the base of her skull intensified, Kara took a silent vow to get in touch with her ex-
husband. But how? Should she call him? No, she decided almost immediately. Writing would be less trying
for them both. Her first impulse was to send a letter
off at once. Yet, she reasoned, the weather was still
extremely cold and unpredictable. She wanted everything to go without a hitch when she introduced Edmund to their little girl. Why not wait until spring?
After all, what was a few more weeks?

Strange how free that decision made her feel, she
reflected.

Kara set the warm bottle on the polished walnut ta-
bletop. "I see you have quite a way with women."

"If you mean I've managed to get this one settled
down, so far so good." Bric gave Kara a small smile.
All the while he'd been soothing Lynn, he'd kept an
eye on her mother and hadn't missed that faraway
look in her eyes. He couldn't help wondering what had
put it there.

"I can take her now," Kara offered.

"No, let me." Still cradling Lynn in the crook of an
arm, Bric reached for her bottle. As the baby sucked
greedily, he enthused, "She has some appetite."

"When she's partway through, you should try to
burp her. Better take this towel to protect your shirt."

He waved away the terry cloth Kara held out. "No
need. What's a little milk?"

"You might be surprised," she warned.

A short while later, he hoisted Lynn over his shoulder. To Bric's dismay, his gentle pats brought up an amazingly loud sound for one so small, followed by a wet trickle down his back.

Kara grabbed the towel and dabbed at the mess her daughter had made.

"How has she grown so much when she doesn't keep down half of what she drinks? That was some geyser."

Kara laughed with Bric. "I've been considering rechristening her. Think Old Faithful would be appropriate?"

With the tip of a finger, Kara turned Bric's face toward her and wiped a small splatter of milk from his cheek. The circular motion slowed, then stopped as his eyes melded with hers. Kara was the first to lower her gaze. Clearing her throat, she improvised, "I think I need a little water."

It would be safer, she concluded as she returned to the living room, to let Bric do his own cleaning up. Kara traded the washcloth for Lynn. While the baby finished her bottle, Bric rubbed at his sodden shirt as best he could.

"I'm afraid I'm not having much luck." He lifted a shoulder and sniffed. "I smell like overripe cottage cheese."

Kara flushed with embarrassment. "Why don't you take that off and let me wash it for you? I have a small washer-dryer in the storage room off the kitchen."

"You don't have to bother," he protested half-heartedly.

"Yes, I do." Kara smiled. "This is a very small apartment." Laying Lynn in her playpen, she held out a squeaky toy. "That should keep her busy for all of two seconds."

When she turned around again, she saw that Bric had taken her at her word and stripped out of the soggy shirt. Kara swallowed hard, unable to tear her eyes away from the swirl of dark hair that covered his chest and disappeared beneath the waistband of his jeans.

It took her a few moments to find her voice. "You're going to be cold."

"Nah, I'm half Eskimo."

Despite his easy tone, her fingers trembled as she reached for the shirt. "I won't be a minute. By the way, the coffee's ready. Help yourself. Cups are on the counter."

When she returned, she was carrying an old shirt Joey had brought from home to use as a paint smock. "I think Mr. Parker's about your size," she said, handing him the garment. As he dubiously eyed the well-splattered oxford cloth, she assured him, "It's only paint."

"What a relief!"

As he put it on, Kara was struck by the intimacy of the moment. It had been a long time since she'd seen a man dress. Suddenly she realized she was staring again and averted her head. Without Lynn as a buffer between them, she felt awkward and frantically searched for something to say.

Bric saved her the trouble. "How are Sam and Delia getting along?" he inquired as he took the seat opposite her and picked up his coffee cup. "Pregnancy giving her any trouble?"

"No, she's fine," Kara informed him, seizing upon the neutral topic. "Except Delia complains Sam won't let her lift a finger. She insists she doesn't need to be treated with kid gloves, but Sam doesn't pay her any mind. Delia tells me she finds it irritating, but I think it's . . . well . . . sweet."

That remote look was back in her eyes, and Bric guessed that she was remembering how vastly different her own pregnancy had been. She'd had no one to take care of her. A sharp pain jabbed at the middle of Bric's chest. He would give anything to have been around so that he could have pampered her, protected her. He reined in that trend of his thoughts and steered his attention back to the conversation.

"If it's a girl, they're going to name her after me," Kara told him between sips of the coffee Bric had poured for her. "Imagine that."

"You sound surprised."

"I am. Islanders have a lot of trouble accepting anyone not born here."

"But you're special."

The way he said the word was very nearly a caress, and Kara stirred uneasily. Suddenly the atmosphere in the small apartment prickled with electricity.

SILHOUETTE®

 PRESENTS

A Real Sweetheart of a Deal!

6
FREE
GIFTS

PEEL BACK THIS CARD AND SEE WHAT YOU CAN GET! THEN...

Complete the Hand Inside

It's easy! To play your cards right, just match this card with the cards inside.

Turn over for more details . . .

Incredible isn't it? Deal yourself in <u>right now</u> and get 6 fabulous gifts. *ABSOLUTELY FREE.*

1. 4 BRAND NEW SILHOUETTE SPECIAL EDITION® NOVELS— FREE!
Sit back and enjoy the excitement, romance and thrills of four fantastic novels. You'll receive them as part of this winning streak!

2. A BEAUTIFUL AND PRACTICAL CLOCK/CALENDAR—FREE
You'll love this lucite Digital Quartz Clock — a handsome addition to any decor! The changeable month-at-a-glance calendar pops out and can be replaced with your favourite photograph.

3. AN EXCITING MYSTERY BONUS—FREE!
And still your luck holds! You'll also receive a special mystery bonus. You'll be thrilled with this surprise gift. It is elegant as well as practical.

PLUS

THERE'S MORE. THE DECK IS STACKED IN YOUR FAVOUR. HERE ARE TWO MORE WINNING POINTS. YOU'LL ALSO RECEIVE:

4. MONEY SAVING HOME DELIVERY
Imagine how you'll enjoy having the chance to preview the romantic adventures of our Silhouette heroines in the convenience of your own home! Here's how it works. Every month we'll deliver 6 new Silhouette Special Edition novels right to your door. There's no obligation to buy, and if you decide to keep them, they'll be yours for only $2.49* each! That's 26 cents below the cover price, plus only 69 cents for postage and handling for the entire shipment!

5. MORE GIFTS FROM TIME TO TIME—FREE!
It's easy to see why you have the winning hand. In addition to all the other special deals available only to our home subscribers, when you join Silhouette Books, you can look forward to additional free gifts throughout the year.

SO DEAL YOURSELF IN – YOU CAN'T HELP BUT WIN

* Terms and Prices subject to change.

Bric sensed her discomfort and backed off. He knew he was pushing, but around Kara he found it hard not to. While they waited for the washer-dryer to complete its cycle, he directed their talk toward generalities. At last he remarked, "I'd better head home before it gets dark."

"Of course. I'll get your shirt."

"I've enjoyed this afternoon," he observed after she'd handed it to him.

"So have I. You're welcome here anytime, Bric."

He stopped at the playpen and skimmed a palm over Lynn's downy head. "Bye, little Miss Vesuvius." Rewarded with a broad, toothless smile, he bent to kiss the tip of her nose, then turned to catch Kara blinking back tears.

During the past weeks, Bric had convinced himself that if he couldn't have Kara Reynolds in any other way, at least he could have her for a friend. But as he stood gazing down at her, he admitted he wanted more than friendship. Much more.

Unable to help himself, he reached out and drew her to him, lowering his mouth over hers.

Degree by degree, the kiss went from undemanding to inviting to searing. Before Kara knew what she was doing, her hands had found their way around his neck, tugging him closer. Knocked completely off balance by the heated persuasion of his lips, she held on, never wanting to let go.

She felt the thud of his heart, heard the harshness of his breathing, tasted the heat of his mouth. Though her senses were spinning out of control, she detected a warning voice in a distant corner of her brain. At first faint, it gathered force until it became a relentless chant.

"Bric," she whispered, breaking contact, "this is crazy."

Drawing a deep breath, he gradually loosened his hold. Though he understood Kara's doubts about getting further involved, he knew she was attracted to him. Why else would she respond so spontaneously every time his lips met hers? Maybe it was selfish, but he wanted her. No man, not even her dead husband, could feel for Kara what he felt.

Bric wasn't sure when the subtle change had taken place, but he was no longer willing to settle for a temporary relationship. With Kara, it had to be something far more permanent.

But convincing her that they were right for each other would be no easy matter, he knew. Kara wanted more children, and he couldn't give them to her. Somehow he had to make her see that he wouldn't really be depriving her of a family. After all, she did have Lynn.

He'd have to make her love him so much she forgot about giving her daughter a brother or sister. But that was going to take time. And patience. She would have be very sure of her choice. Otherwise, she'd only grow to resent him. If Bric wanted to win her, he'd have to give her room. He prayed that he could hold himself in check long enough for Kara to come to him. And if she didn't? He couldn't think of that, or he'd go crazy.

Bric again hauled her close for one last kiss. "I'll be back," he promised before releasing her.

After he'd gone, Kara leaned against the door and closed her eyes. If the rate of her pulse was any indication, she was in deeper than she thought. Yet how could she trust her judgment...especially with the emotional tug-of-war going on inside her.

Wise or not, Kara saw a lot of Bric during the next week. It seemed that whenever he could spare time from his busy schedule, he flew to Perry's Island, where he found dozens of odd jobs that needed attention in her apartment and classroom. He'd told Kara that carpentry was his hobby, but she was both surprised and pleased at his design for a reading table he planned to turn out for her students. Joey was especially fascinated by Bric's toolbox and inevitably found a reason to be at his side.

That was exactly where Kara found her first grader on Friday after school. Bric was teaching him the names of various tools and demonstrating how to use them. It wasn't long before Joey was practicing away by hammering a large nail into a two-by-four.

Kara leaned against the doorpost and beamed approvingly at the tall man and little boy so intent on their work. How good Bric was for Joey, she reflected. Not condescending or patronizing, but patient and caring.

Bric suddenly looked up and caught Kara's eye. Time seemed to stand still as the two of them clung to the moment. Before he turned back to his work, Bric sent her a look that had her nipples beading with want. Kara stood transfixed, her gaze playing over the rippling muscles that pulled Bric's blue work shirt tight across his shoulders. She remembered the feel of that firm body pressed to hers and had an irrational urge to fling herself into his arms and drag his mouth to her hungry lips. Instead, she watched Joey as he drove the nail in perfectly straight, earning a pat on the back and words of praise.

Then Bric covered the boy's hand to teach him the proper way to sand with the grain of wood. As though Bric's roughened hands were enveloping hers, Kara's fingertips tingled with imagined warmth. Abruptly she swiveled and returned to her apartment. Later she heard Bric compliment the smooth surface Joey had produced on the practice board. When Joey had replied, his voice had been bursting with boyish pride. No wonder the six-year-old worshiped the man.

And what about her? Wasn't she even more bedazzled?

"Mrs. Reynolds! Mrs. Reynolds!" Joey flew into Kara's kitchen. "Know what? Me and Mr. Brickner's gonna build a snowman. Wanna help?"

"Mr. Brickner and *I*, Joey," she said with a wry smile.

"Whatever," the excited child gushed. "You comin'?"

"I'd love to, dear, but it's time for Lynn's bottle. Maybe later, after she goes to sleep. Tell you what, I'll scour up a hat and scarf for Mr. Snowman."

"Okay. We'll build him right outside there, so you can see," he said and scampered off.

Kara moved her rocker to the window and followed Bric and Joey's progress while Lynn drained her bottle. Afterward she held her daughter up and waved her tiny hand at the two outside. Kara was amused as Joey gleefully showed off, dancing around like a loose-jointed puppet.

When Lynn's eyes began to droop, Kara put the sleepy baby to bed and got ready to join in the outdoor fun. After changing into a bulky sweater and slacks, she dashed to the door. At the last minute she remembered the cap and scarf she'd promised Joey.

By the time she got outside, the two were already fashioning stone eyes, nose and mouth on their three-tiered figure. "I timed that right, didn't I?" Kara plopped the stocking cap on the snowman's head and swirled the knit scarf around the neck. "You guys did all the hard work, and I deliver the finishing touches."

"Think you're smart, don't you, teacher?" Bric goaded her. "But I know a good way to wipe that smug expression off your pretty face." Grinning, he leaned down and scooped up a handful of snow.

"Oh, no, you don't!" Kara shrieked, quickly arming herself and taking aim.

"A snowball fight!" Joey shouted.

Bric nailed Kara on the shoulder, while she scored a direct hit squarely in Bric's face.

As he whisked wet crystals from his eyes with one hand, he grabbed a fistful of snow with the other. "I thought you said you didn't have a good arm. Where did you learn to throw like that?" he shot back, synchronizing words with action.

"From my dad. He always wanted to be a Reds pitcher," she crowed, ducking as the snowball buzzed by her head.

Thanks to Joey's rapid volley, Bric was momentarily distracted, and once again her missile found its target directly in the center of his chest.

"Bull's-eye!" she whooped. "Great diversionary tactic, Joey."

"Spoken too soon," Bric warned as she whirled right into the shot Joey got off.

"I thought you were on my side," Kara grumbled good-naturedly.

"It's every man for himself," Bric decreed, rapidly firing snowballs at the other two.

The next fifteen minutes were sheer bedlam as the three alternately hurled and dodged white weapons. Finally, in a fit of desperation, Joey tackled Bric, who rolled to the ground, taking the boy with him. In seconds they both looked as though they'd fallen into a flour bin.

Laughing, Kara pounced forward and landed on top of the heap. "Who said the Abominable Snowman was a myth? I've just caught myself two of the critters!'' she squealed, stubbornly hanging on as the captives tried to topple her.

In the midst of their laughing free-for-all, they were taken by surprise when a shrill voice gibed, ''Joey Engel, what do you think you're doing?''

Edith Parker marched militantly into the school yard. After jerking her nephew upright, she brushed furiously at his snow-mantled coat. ''So this is where you were! You're going to catch your death of cold. Do you know that, boy? As for you—'' she glared at Bric and Kara, who were still smiling as they scrambled to their feet ''—I never expected such carryings on!''

As soon as his aunt's anger shifted to Kara and Bric, Joey brought up his chin. ''It ain't . . . isn't their fault, Aunt Edith. I asked to build the snowman.''

''You're nothing but trouble, boy. Now there'll be a doctor bill to pay and medicine to buy. As if we didn't have enough expenses already.''

While Kara cringed at the cutting words, Bric stepped forward and dropped a hand on Joey's shoulder. ''Wait a minute, sport—you can't take all the credit. I was the one who threw the first snowball.''

''Well, I never!'' In pulling herself erect, Mrs. Parker overcompensated and landed in an unseemly sprawl on her backside.

Kara and Joey bent over solicitously and helped Bric haul her up. After a hurried inspection to be certain she wasn't hurt, Bric noted, ''Why, Mrs. Parker, I believe you've made a butterfly in the snow." He pointed out how the imprint of her wide bottom formed the body, the brush of her wool coat the wings and the outline of her shoes the head and antenna.

Though Kara considered it a sad-looking insect at best, Edith Parker seemed rather pleased. Recovering her dignity, she tugged at her coat, setting it straight. "Why, so I have!"

"Now wasn't that fun?"

"I'm not sure I'd go so far as to say that. But I guess all's well that end's well!"

Bric laughed at her unexpected show of humor. "I couldn't have put it better myself. Honestly, Mrs. Parker, I'm sorry if I led Joey astray, but we were only having some innocent fun."

"Innocent, you say! It's more the kind that makes a lot of work for a body. But I don't expect you'd know what a parent goes through, being single and all."

The comment stung, but Bric kept his face expressionless. What he'd give to have a boy like that, he mused. Slapping the snow off his jeans, he suggested, "I tell you what, Mrs. Parker, if Joey does catch cold, why don't you send me the bill? If anyone's at fault here, I am."

Mollified, Edith softened a bit. "Thanks all the same, Mr. Brickner, but we can manage. I expect Joey'll be all right. He don't appear chilled."

"Friends, then?" Bric held out his hand, and Mrs. Parker gave it a weak squeeze. Before they left, Kara added her apologies to Bric's and promised to keep better track of the time when Joey stayed after school. Then she leaned over and whispered in the boy's ear.

When the two were on their way, Bric asked, "What did you say to make Joey's eyes light up like that?"

Kara linked her arm in his as they strolled back to the apartment. "I told him he was manly to want to shoulder the blame. And that I was proud of him."

Bric stopped to tilt up her chin. "Have I told you lately that you're wonderful?"

"Have I returned the compliment?"

"I mean it, Kara."

"So do I. You handled Edith Parker exactly right. And you're terrific with Joey. The kind of role model he needs."

Bric gave her a warm smile. "Does that mean I rate a hot cup of coffee?"

"More than that." Caging his face, she drew his mouth to hers.

Chapter Eight

A steady March rain buffeted the schoolhouse, transforming the yard outside into a slushy moat—and Kara's students into holy terrors. For the past hour, Billy Oldt had been jumping up and down like an overwound jack-in-the-box. Even the normally placid Ruth was fidgeting in her seat.

Kara sighed. Why fight it? She might as well capitalize on being superintendent, principal and teacher rolled into one.

"Okay, everybody," she decreed, "I'm going to put you out of your misery. Let's close the books and call it a day."

The announcement was no sooner out of her mouth

when Billy let out a whoop that would have done a rebel soldier proud.

"Watch it, young man, or I may make an exception in your case."

"Aw, Mrs. Reynolds, if you keep me late, I might have to swim home. That'd be cruel and unusual punishment."

"Don't tempt me," Kara warned, biting back a smile. "Now, be sure to put on your boots, everybody. It's really soupy out there."

Kara didn't even try to prevent their mad rush for the cloakroom. Propping an elbow on the desk and shielding her face with a palm, she rewarded herself with a few moments of quiet.

Almost at once an image of Bric pushed into her consciousness. These days, thoughts of him often leaped to mind. Since their snowball fight and the kiss that had followed, Kara had battled conflicting emotions. It wasn't fair, she reminded herself time after time, to lead Bric on when she wasn't certain how far she was prepared to carry their relationship.

Yet where he was concerned, she seemed to have no control. It was as if she'd been torn in two. While her intellect advised her to discourage him, her heart whispered something far different.

Kara methodically rubbed her temples. For the millionth time she asked herself what she ought to do. If only she could dismiss Bric as easily as her class! But how could she, when he was practically everything a woman could want? Never had she met a man like him, a man who was as sensitive as he was strong.

Her thoughts turned to the scene Mrs. Parker had witnessed. Not long after, Bric had become the butt of some gentle ribbing at the winery. He'd told Kara that since his seeing her so frequently was providing grist for the gossip mill, he'd better be more discreet and curtail his visits. Not that he cared about himself, he'd asserted, but it was a small community, and he didn't want to subject her to any censure.

Though pleased by Bric's consideration, Kara was also disappointed. She'd started looking forward to seeing him at the close of each school day. Like it or not, she missed Bric when he wasn't around. Before long she was compelled to face a bittersweet truth: she wanted to be with him more than just weekends and the solitary Tuesdays he'd designated to play handyman at the school.

"Do I got to leave?" a small voice pleaded beside her.

Opening her eyes, Kara found Joey clutching his lunch box and boots. He'd slid only one arm into his coat, leaving an empty sleeve to dangle on the floor. His expression was so woebegone that she reached out and drew him to her side. "Don't you want to go home, Joey?"

"Not yet. It's Tuesday. I always help Mr. Brickner on Tuesdays."

Kara tipped her head toward the window, frowning. "I'm not sure he'll be able to come today, Joey."

Was it that uncertainty—more than her restless students—that had given her a pounding headache?

"But he promised. We're going to make Aunt Edith a napkin holder. For her birthday. We gotta get started, 'cause it's on April 29."

Kara brushed a shock of hair off Joey's forehead. "The weather's kind of bad, honey."

"It's only a little rain."

"But what if the temperature should drop? It's liable to turn to snow this time of year. We wouldn't want Mr. Brickner to fly home in a bad storm, would we?"

"Suppose not." Joey's lower lip came out in a pout.

"Don't worry." Kara gave him a reassuring squeeze. "There's more than a month before your aunt's birthday. Mr. Brickner won't forget."

"Forget what?" a deep voice inquired.

Joey's lunch box and boots slipped from his hands. With his coat half trailing behind him, he dashed headlong toward the tall figure filling the doorway. "You came!"

"Would I let you down, pal?" Bric asked, stooping to catch Joey in his arms.

Tears sprang to Kara's eyes as she watched him fold Joey in a quick hug. Over the top of the six-year-old's head, her eyes found his.

You're so good with him, Kara's said.

It's my pleasure, his returned.

For several seconds neither spoke. But no words were needed to explain the warm feelings that flowed between them. All at once Kara felt herself taking a mental step in Bric's direction, but Joey broke the mood.

"Mrs. Reynolds said you might not come 'cause of the rain. She said it might get too bad for you to fly tonight."

"She did, did she?" he commented, helping the boy off with his coat. "I thought she knew me better than that." Again Bric's eyes sought Kara's and telegraphed a clear message. *Remember the night Lynn was born?*

She smiled. "I'd forgotten Mr. Brickner likes to court danger."

"What's that mean?" Joey asked, looking from one to the other.

"Never mind, sport. Help me pick up these papers and push the desks back in place. Then we'll get busy on that present for your aunt."

"Looks like a cyclone hit the room today, doesn't it?" Kara observed. "While you two straighten up, I'll see if Mrs. McCann wouldn't like to start home. Before you begin sawing away, how about stopping by the kitchen for some cake? My way of saying thanks for tackling this mess."

A few minutes later Bric went into Kara's apartment, where he saw that Mrs. McCann was just buttoning her coat. "Go on inside," she urged him. "Lynn's awake."

Softly closing the bedroom door behind him, Bric sneaked up on Kara, who was bent over the baby. He swung his arms around her waist and pulled her against him murmuring, "About that thank you. I'll take the first installment now."

Though common sense cautioned Kara to hold back, her body had a different idea. Unable to resist his touch, she turned and looped her arms around his neck. "I'm paying in installments, am I? Does that mean you expect interest?"

"I'm not mercenary," he claimed with mock indignation. "Except when it comes to you." His mouth trailed leisurely over her face, sending tiny quivers chasing through her. "I can't seem to get enough of you, woman. Do you know it's been two whole days since our last kiss? Which makes you delinquent in your daily payments."

"Hardly my fault," she said breathily. "You weren't here to collect."

"Not out of choice, sweet. Besides your good name to protect, I have this Simon Legree for a partner. Would you believe he expects me to put in equal time?"

"That's right. Blame it on poor Mark," Kara teased him.

The arch of her neck invited Bric to spread kisses along the delicate curve of her jaw. His lips registered an excited throbbing at her pulse point that had him moaning in satisfaction.

"Hey," Kara murmured in a silky voice, "when I promised a treat, I didn't realize I was on the menu. But two can play this game, wouldn't you say?" As she found his mouth, she bit into his lower lip and sucked lightly. "Hmm, sweeter than the icing on my cake."

"Lady, you ain't tasted nothing yet!" He brought his mouth down hard on hers in a kiss that went on and on. It seemed as if he couldn't get close enough to satisfy the raw yearning that already had his heart drumming furiously. His hands rode over the swell of her breasts, then down and under her sweater.

She flattened her palms against his back to urge him nearer. It felt so good, so right, to be in Bric's arms. For a while time ceased to exist, and she lost herself in the taste and feel of him, in the mindless joy of his lips moving over hers.

"Mrs. Reynolds! Are you in there?"

Joey's summons rudely forced them apart. As Bric's mouth left hers, he groaned, "The patter of little feet is already heavy around here, and Lynn can't even walk yet."

They took a moment to steady their breathing before Kara called, "I'll be right there, Joey."

For the remainder of the afternoon, Bric and Joey measured and sawed in a corner of the classroom. Joey was so excited about surprising his crusty aunt that no sooner had he completed one step than he was ready to take on the next. Bric even began to worry that he wouldn't have time to give Kara more than a quick goodbye kiss.

A glance outside only added to his anxiety. The strong wind that had whipped up in the past hour was lashing sheets of rain against the windows. He knew he should head out soon, before the weather grew any worse. *Damn!* Today even the elements seemed to be against him.

He clenched his jaw in frustration. The memory of that brief interlude when he'd taken Kara in his arms was still playing merry hell with his libido. He'd promised himself to let her come to him, but how was that possible when they rarely had a private moment?

Though his restraint was perilously close to snapping, Bric couldn't bring himself to call a halt for the day, not when Joey was enjoying himself so much. At last, a phone message from Mrs. Parker spared Bric the necessity.

Kara eased Joey's hesitant departure by tucking several homemade chocolate cookies into his lunch box. "For after dinner. Now, don't forget to stop by the Oldts' for the cup of cornmeal your aunt wants," she reminded him before sending him on his way with a hug.

"Poor little fellow," she told Bric, who stood by the kitchen sink, washing his hands. "He's starved for love."

"I know the feeling." His tone barely masked his growing impatience.

Deliberately slighting the remark, Kara pretended to watch Joey's progress down the road. "Oh, no!" she suddenly gasped. "It's sleeting!"

Bric heard the first pellets of ice strike the glass panes. "As much as I hate to, I'd better take off," he said, pivoting toward the classroom to retrieve his coat.

"Not in this!"

"If I hurry, I'll be home before it really gets nasty."

"No!" she countered. "Don't take the chance. Stay here tonight." The offer spilled out before she stopped to consider how he might interpret it.

Bric froze in the middle of slipping into his jacket. Kara's concern for his safety touched him deeply. Yet he felt it only fair to warn her that if he spent the night, it might end differently than the one on Mahler's. Looking her squarely in the eye, he contended, "If I do, I'm not sure—"

"You can take the couch. Actually, it's pretty comfortable. Or I can sleep out here and you can have my bed—if you don't think Lynn will disturb you."

"Peace wasn't uppermost in my mind."

Kara's cheeks colored. "Talk's cheap," she chided him, and whirled around to check the contents of her cabinets. Little by little, she realized, they'd come to fall back on a suggestive playfulness whenever the sexual tension became unbearable, but tonight Kara sensed the rules were about to change.

Unnerved, she chattered on while she fixed spaghetti. "Joey's been so excited about making that napkin holder. It's quite a project for a little boy."

"True, but Joey's a quick learner. After we finish this, I'll let him help me with the stove flue. It could stand cleaning, and I don't imagine the school board will get around to thinking about it until summer."

"You've done far too much already," Kara protested, bringing their filled plates to the table.

Grinning, Bric seated her before taking his place. "But it's such a good excuse to come see you."

"Is that so? You don't fool anyone. As you well know, we're the talk of the island."

"Does it bother you?" he probed.

"No." No, she realized with sudden insight, it didn't bother her at all.

While she and Bric satisfied a physical appetite with dinner, their meaningful glances and casual touches slowly whetted another kind of hunger.

They were finishing the cake Kara had served after school when Bric noticed a smidgen of white frosting at the corner of her mouth. Capturing her chin between his thumb and forefinger, he leaned over and carefully lifted the icing onto his tongue, then raised his head to stare into her eyes. Minutes ticked by while their surroundings gradually seemed to dissolve. With agonizing slowness, he inched his lips toward hers.

Passions that had been smoldering for weeks suddenly exploded in a mind-stealing kiss. His greedy mouth on hers released a floodgate in Kara, toppling the world on its axis as pleasure spiraled through her. She was hardly aware when he put his hands under her arms and eased her to her feet.

Somehow she and Bric ended up on the couch, their bodies fused as tightly as their mouths. He slipped his hands beneath her sweater to caress her bare back. Carried away on a tide of emotion, Kara melted into him. Excitement skated along her spine. She plowed her fingers into his hair to draw him nearer. His faintly musky smell filled her nostrils, making her want him with a need so overpowering it terrified her.

Before she realized it, Bric had taken off her sweater, and only her filmy bra separated her breasts from his touch. As his hands roamed over the feminine curves that shaped the nylon, Kara felt her nipples thrust tautly, painfully against the sheer fabric.

Once more his mouth sought hers. This time he savored her with a gentleness that shattered the last vestige of Kara's reserve, rousing her with a quiet persuasion that left every nerve ending trembling with desire. As the kiss grew more urgent, her fingers found the buttons of his shirt and worked them free.

When Bric's mouth finally left hers, he lowered the silk bra straps off her shoulders, drinking in the sight of her bare breasts. "Breathtaking. I knew you would be," he said shakily as his palms cupped the creamy mounds.

"Too small," she countered.

"No. See how perfectly you fill my hands?" He kneaded the soft skin, then rolled first one, then the other coral-tipped bud between his fingers, making the already hardened peaks unbearably sensitive.

Kara gasped as his lips followed his fingers. At the teasing flicks of his tongue, a rush of heat shafted through her, turning her insides to molten lava.

Without her realizing how, the rest of her clothes fell away. When Bric again lowered himself upon her, she took his full weight as his demanding mouth located her lips, her cheeks, her neck. Afloat on sensations she'd never before experienced, she spun into a world of boundless emotion. All thought, all worry, all inhibitions evaporated, and for the first time in her life she felt truly alive as a woman. She no longer questioned the rightness of making love with Bric. She felt drawn to him by a force she was powerless to contest. They seemed fated to come together. With a boldness that was new to her, she impatiently fumbled with the snap of his jeans.

Bric had been determined to keep the pace slow, but Kara's ready response was making that next to impossible. She made him burn. He raised himself just enough to wriggle out of his clothes. A shudder tore through him as her shapely legs twined around his bare body, her delving fingers plowed through his hair, her parted lips scattered frantic kisses over the planes and angles of his face.

Holding back nothing, giving everything, Kara stirred in Bric a deep yearning. She made him desire her with a fierceness that shook his very soul.

As her hands moved over his chest, he covered her mouth with his. He demanded at the same time that he satisfied. With his tongue he compellingly traced the line separating her lips until they opened for his possession. Simultaneously his fingers sought the core of her womanhood, imitating the movement of his tongue.

Bric's intimate touch sent a liquid warmth surging through Kara. His whispered encouragement had her reaching for him, caressing him. With a groan, he trailed his lips down her throat to her breasts. Kara leaned into his strength, certain there could be nothing more agonizingly sweet than this erotic assault on her senses. She'd never been so crazed.

Why? asked a tiny voice at the back of her mind.

Because... because, she heard another affirm, *you're in love.*

Suddenly it didn't matter to Kara whether or not she and Bric had a future together. All that counted was how she felt, what she felt. She loved Bric, whose mouth and hands even now were igniting flames that licked along her veins.

He eased into her with exquisite tenderness. When his rhythmic thrusts quickened, deepened, Kara moved with him, soaring upward to a pinnacle of sensation beyond anything in her wildest fantasies. Her inner center swelled, tightened, coiled. All her attention was concentrated on that spot alone when unexpectedly a violent spasm shook her. Kara called out Bric's name as tremor after tremor shuddered through her body. Riding the aftershocks, she clung desperately to him, barely aware of his fulfilling release.

Totally spent, Kara allowed her eyes to drift closed. Minutes later—or was it hours?—she opened them. At first she imagined she'd been dreaming. But no. She was lying on her side with Bric's arm flung across her hip. There was just enough room for Kara to twist onto her back and stretch.

When a low, sultry sound hummed in her throat, Bric rasped, "My sentiments exactly." He brushed aside a strand of reddish-brown hair to feather a kiss at her temple.

Kara sighed and again closed her eyes. She was enormously grateful to Bric. He'd liberated feelings she'd long held in check, feelings she'd been afraid to express. She rolled over to face him. "Thank you," she breathed throatily.

"The pleasure was all mine."

"No, it wasn't. That is, I . . ." Kara hesitated, all at once shy about revealing what was on her mind.

"What?" Bric quietly prodded her.

"I never felt that way before."

"It was terrific for me, too."

"It was more than that for me." She dropped her forehead to his shoulder. "Good heavens, this is so awkward. Why did I have to bring it up?"

Framing her face in his hands, he tipped her head back, "Are you trying to tell me you've never felt the earth move?"

"What a tactful way to put it."

"Oh, Kara, do you know how special that makes me feel?" His voice cracked with emotion.

Bric ran his fingertips lightly up and down her skin. Questions about her husband briefly flitted into his mind, but he shunted them aside as he reveled in the warmth of her confession. "I wanted it to be good for you. And I'm glad it was. I was afraid it wouldn't be—I wanted you so much I had trouble holding back."

"You weren't alone," she admitted with an embarrassed flush.

He kissed the tip of her nose. "I noticed. And it excited me."

She cuddled closer, unreasonably pleased with herself. In no time, though, her arms began to go numb. "I hate to complain, but isn't it a little cramped here? I vote we move while we still can."

"What did you have in mind, love?"

"I don't think Lynn will object if you share my bed."

He grinned, then dropped a kiss on the top of her head. "I thought you'd never ask."

Seven inches of wet, heavy snow followed the sleet. So terrible were conditions by the following morning that Kara decided to declare a school holiday. She told herself it wasn't so much to save the embarrassment of having Mrs. McCann find Bric at her breakfast table as to give her and the children a needed break. Besides, according to the seven-thirty news, school had been canceled on the other islands, so why shouldn't she make it unanimous?

Fortunately, the phone lines weren't down, so she was able to reach all the students. After feeding Lynn, she went back to wake Bric.

He was sleeping peacefully, his arms outside the quilt, his face shadowed by the rough stubble of his dark beard. For a long time, she stood in the door-way, watching him, reflecting on what they had shared. His lovemaking had shown her she wasn't, as she had so long feared, inadequate as a woman. Whatever else, Kara would always be grateful to him for giving her back her femininity.

Last night she'd opened her body to him as he'd once opened his soul to her. Remembering, she felt a twinge of guilt. She, too, harbored a secret. Sooner or later she would have to bring it out into the light. But not now. Now was for something more enjoyable.

Kara slid off her robe and got into bed. Rolling to one side, she tucked a hand under her head and with the other traced the swirling pattern of dark hair across Bric's chest.

His eyes opened and tracked the movement of her fingers. With a sideways look, he asked in a husky voice, "What do you think you're doing?"

"Checking you for scars. I love that one on your cheek."

"Is that right?"

"Mm-hmm. Ever had your appendix out?"

"Want to see for yourself?" With an unsteady hand, he tossed aside the covers, unable to believe how much he wanted her again. Desire throbbed in his veins, stoking a smoldering need that at any second threatened to burst into flame.

A shiver trembled through him as her tongue slipped along his jawline and down the hard column of his neck. "Feel free to investigate all you like," he said thickly. "But for your information, my appendix is lower."

Encouraged by his response, Kara felt heady with power. It thrilled her to be able to stir him this way. She lay with the upper part of her body over his, taking pleasure in the feel of his springy chest hair against her already erect nipples. "I'm working my way there," she purred, sweeping her hands down his muscled flanks. "You're so magnificent. All man."

He held his breath, then spoke. "I can't make you pregnant, Kara. I can't ever be a father." Bric couldn't avoid a painful comparison with her husband. The man might have been an indifferent lover, but he'd been whole, potent. Able to give Kara what Bric himself never could.

At the bleak expression that clouded his face, Kara gripped his shoulders. "Let's not waste precious time talking."

"Time?" Bric sprang upright, his glance darting to the bedside clock. "Good Lord, Kara! Have you lost your mind? The kids'll be arriving at school any minute."

She shoved him back on the bed. "Relax. I called off school. So the kids . . . and we, can play." Her fingers found him and made certain he didn't mistake her meaning.

"Kara, what you do to me!" With a shudder, he reached for her hands. "Enough, woman. I can't take any more."

"Sensitive?" she taunted him as her lips meandered over the firm muscles of his torso.

"Temptress!" On a ragged moan, Bric flipped Kara over and blanketed her body with his. Hungrily his lips fastened to hers for a deep, passionate kiss.

As her mouth opened, Bric softened the pressure. He savored her sweet flavor even as his hands memorized the graceful lines of her body. His lips charted a moist path along her jaw and down her neck. By the time he reached the sensitive hollow at the base, her pulse was hammering wildly.

Kara's head fell back. She lost herself beneath Bric's demanding hands and mouth. Her every cell responded with unbearable sensitivity to his slightest touch. She breathed his name again and again as desire wound ever more tightly within her.

"So, so beautiful," Bric praised her, cupping one swollen breast and rubbing a callused thumb over the taut peak. When he took it in his mouth and gently suckled, Kara moaned, her fingers diving into his thick, dark hair. It was glorious to be wanted so much.

She quivered when he shifted slightly to treat her other breast to equal pleasure. "I never knew it could be so wonderful," she marveled.

"This is only the beginning." He lowered his head so that he could dip his tongue into her navel. Kara pulled in a sharp breath when his lips trailed even farther downward.

His mouth and fingers took her soaring over snow-covered pines into a fierce white storm. Lost in a blizzard of whirling sensations, Kara dug her nails into his shoulders and struggled upward toward the sun. All at once its blinding light shattered her universe into a prism of colors. With a cry, she relaxed and languidly floated back to earth.

Bric hardly gave her time to recover before he joined their bodies. His hands came under her head, lifting it to once again fuse their lips. Reflexively, she dug her nails into his muscled buttocks and urged him to take her to an even higher peak than before. Just when Kara thought there could be no more zeniths to scale, Bric taught her differently.

They had only begun.

Chapter Nine

As Bric eased the car in beside the curb, Kara rolled down her window and gaped. The house wasn't at all what she'd expected. She had thought Bric would've preferred something sleek and modern, rather like the snazzy black sports car she was sitting in. Instead, rising three stories before her was a sprawling Victorian monolith.

Kara noticed how the massive old dwelling dominated its neighbors along the wide, tree-lined street. Smiling, she enthused, "Character. Lots of character. Oh, Bric, it's wonderful!"

Bric fairly leaped from the low-slung car, his wide grin attesting to how pleased he was at her reaction. For weeks he'd been wanting to show Kara his house, but before last Tuesday he'd put off inviting her. He wasn't sure if she'd invent an excuse, and he didn't relish facing the disappointment.

After skirting the hood, he opened the passenger door to lift Lynn into his arms and help Kara out. "I'm glad you like it. Here, you carry Merry Sunshine while I get the bags."

"Merry Sunshine? I thought you'd christened her Miss Vesuvius—for christening you."

"Very funny!"

Kara laughed. "Actually, Sunshine's more appropriate. She's such a cheerful baby."

"Why shouldn't she be? Look who she has for a mother."

"Thanks. I'll remind her you said that when she's a teenager."

As Bric gathered their things from the trunk, Kara surveyed the house. She guessed it had been built around the turn of the century, but the dark red bricks looked newly pointed, their deep tone enriched by an off-white trim.

As Kara mounted the steps of the L-shaped porch, she speculated about Bric's reasons for having purchased such an enormous place. It certainly wasn't the typical bachelor pad. More like a home for the family in *Cheaper by the Dozen*. Of course, he'd said he wanted her to meet someone. Could it be that another person shared this huge old house with him? In the time she'd known Bric, he'd mentioned only one close friend—Mark Carlisle—and she'd already met him.

Bric got the door, and Kara walked into a formal entry hall. Eggshell-colored wallpaper with a small burgundy print, an exquisite parquet floor and a magnificent stained glass window set off the walnut stairway that angled gracefully upward and out of sight. A quick glance to the left told Kara that the living-room furnishings were a comfortable blend of Victorian and traditional. Flanking the mantle were two rosewood chairs, their dark green velvet upholstery and serpentine lines strikingly dignified.

"I'm speechless!" Kara admitted when her eyes ceased their excited wandering and returned to Bric. "It's fabulous!"

"Johnny, is that you?" A tall, pleasant-looking woman in her late forties trailed into the hall, a tea towel draped over one arm. "Oh," she continued, not giving Bric a chance to answer, "you must be Kara." She caught a strand of dark, silver-streaked hair that had escaped from the knot on top of her head and pinned it in place.

The first thing Kara noticed was her eyes. Brown like Bric's, they twinkled with the barest suggestion of mischief. Her nose was long and slightly irregular, her mouth a tad wide, but the overall effect worked. It was an arresting face. Strong, open, loving.

"Kara, this is my sister Pam. She's offered to babysit so I can take you out for an afternoon and evening on the town. I hired her because she comes so highly recommended by her six kids." He banded his sister's waist and hugged her off balance. "She hasn't a single major fault, other than helping overpopulate the world."

Pam reared back. "What do you mean *fault*? I always considered it fun."

"Having babies or making them?"

"Brat!" Pam gibed, and gave Bric's nose a sharp tweak.

"I love it when you call me names."

Kara watched the affectionate exchange with a mixture of amusement and envy. The two obviously shared a special bond, a rare closeness. For a moment she felt like an outsider, and she was reminded of what she'd missed by never having had a sibling.

"Mind your manners," Pam admonished, wagging her finger in her brother's face. "I still have a pretty wicked backhand." She raised her fist in mock warning.

With a laugh, Bric released her. "Since when? You couldn't even make a spanking sting."

"So I'm opposed to corporal punishment on principle. He can't censure me for a virtue, can he?" she challenged, bringing Kara into the byplay. As Pam hooked an arm around Kara's shoulder, she lifted Lynn's blanket. "Let me get a look at that little doll. Lynn—isn't that what Johnny said you call her?"

"That's right," Kara affirmed, handing her baby into Pam's waiting arms.

"It's been a while since this family's seen anything so little," Pam cooed, undoing the ties on an angora bonnet. "Johnny, why don't you take Kara's coat and show her to her room? Meanwhile, I'll get us a snack in the kitchen."

"Yes, Mother." Bric laughed good-humoredly. For as long as he could remember his older sister had enjoyed ordering him around. But he seldom took offense at her bossiness. In many ways he was closer to Pam than any other member of his family.

"Sorry," Pam tossed over a shoulder as she breezed toward the back of the house. "I sometimes forget my baby brother's over thirty."

"Don't let her intimidate you," Bric whispered into Kara's ear as they climbed the elegant staircase. "She's really all heart."

"I like Pam. Did you see how Lynn went to her without a murmur? You know how she usually objects when strangers want to hold her."

"Smart young lady. Takes after her mother."

At the top of the steps, Kara rounded on him. "Just what are you getting at?"

"Only that I sensed some initial reserve on your part. I, on the other hand, was immediately smitten." His hand snaked around her waist to haul her against him.

Kara poked a recently manicured nail into his ribs. "That must have been before you discovered how pregnant I was. I can still see that look of stunned surprise on your face."

Locking her next to his hip, he led them down the carpeted hallway. "Was I that transparent? I didn't think you noticed."

"Oh, I noticed, all right. And more than your face."

"For shame," Bric tsked, his mouth spreading into a smile that carried a hint of desire. "I didn't think pregnant ladies entertained such thoughts."

"You'd be surprised what went through this pregnant lady's mind when you appeared on her doorstep."

"How about a demonstration?" he suggested huskily as he directed her into a spacious bedroom. Kara hardly had time to admire the ornately carved rosewood bed before Bric closed the door and scooped her into his arms. Two giant strides and she found herself sprawled on the nubby linen spread.

"Bric! What in the world are you up to?" she demanded breathlessly.

"Can't you guess?" he asked, covering her body with his. "I'm ready for a lesson on your fantasies. Prove to me how good a teacher you are."

"But Pam—what will she think?" Kara struggled to wiggle out from beneath him, but she only succeeded in arousing him further.

"Maybe this will convince my domineering sister that I really am all grown-up. Anyway, with Lynn to keep her company, I doubt she'll even miss us."

When Kara's mouth opened in astonished protest, he effectively swallowed her half-hearted objection. It was only a matter of seconds before the kiss went from persuasive to ravenous. Frantically Kara pushed her hands beneath Bric's jacket to bring his warmth closer to hers.

Their lovemaking grew almost primitive, matching the fierceness of their need. In their haste, they didn't bother to dispense with all their clothes before Bric brought them together in a swift culmination of passion. Exhausted, they collapsed side by side until their breathing became regular.

"I can't keep my hands off you," Bric confessed, folding Kara in his arms and rimming her forehead with tender kisses.

"Hmm." She sighed contentedly. "Nice."

"Only an appetizer," he promised. "Much, much too fast. But I'll make it up to you tonight." She looked delightfully disheveled, her dark russet hair spread out temptingly on the wheat-colored pillow. He kissed each corner of her mouth, then released her. "I guess we'd better get downstairs before Pam has Lynn spoiled rotten."

Hurriedly they put twisted clothes to rights and smoothed telltale wrinkles. As Kara neatly tucked her mauve blouse in place, her eyes traveled over the sumptuous room. A walnut bureau, a marble-topped table, two slipper chairs and an upholstered rocker completed the furnishings.

"Is this your room?" Kara asked.

"Yes. I modeled it after the Lincoln bedroom in the White House. Do you like it?"

"I love it. But I never suspected you collected antiques. How many other surprises do you have stashed away?"

"Are you complaining?"

"Not on your life. But somehow you never struck me as the least bit Victorian."

"Didn't I now?" Bric flashed her a wicked grin. "But I suspect the good queen was far less reserved in the privacy of her boudoir. Otherwise she and Albert wouldn't have produced such a large brood." Reaching for his jacket, he added more soberly, "Sometimes life moves too fast. I like to hold on to a bit of the past. I grew up in a home like this. A lot of our furniture had been passed down from generation to generation. Other pieces Dad built himself. Everything had to be pretty sturdy to withstand the punishment it took from our big family."

Kara stood before the bureau's full-length mirror and hand combed her hair. "Growing up with brothers and sisters must have been nice."

"Yes, yes, it was."

The undertone of regret told Kara that Bric was thinking of more than his own upbringing. "Do you think Pam will guess what we were doing?"

"If she does, she's polite enough not to mention it."

Kara repaired her lipstick and took one last glimpse in the mirror. "Am I presentable?"

"No." A twinkle lit his eyes. "You're gorgeous."

Bric dodged Kara's retaliatory punch and opened the door. "We'd better go right down. I'll give you the full house tour later."

"But what if Pam asks how I liked my room?"

"Fake it. A few well-chosen superlatives should do the trick."

"Like . . . most uncomfortable, absolutely dreadful, much too small?"

"Bite your tongue, or I'll have to teach it a lesson," he growled.

"Is that a threat?"

"More like a promise." Abruptly he brought his mouth to hers to illustrate.

Downstairs, Bric's sister had installed Lynn in an infant seat. "She's been an absolute angel!" Pam proclaimed as Bric and Kara walked into the kitchen. "How do you like her plastic throne? She looks like a princess propped up there, doesn't she? That thing's practically an antique. Belonged to my oldest. He's nearly thirty. Coffee?"

Kara accepted a cup and sat down on the wooden chair Bric had pulled out. "It was thoughtful of you to bring it along. I was just going to spread out a blanket on the floor."

"No trouble at all. I kept a few things for the grandchildren. Not that I've needed them. I keep hinting, but all in vain." Without missing a beat, she veered off on another subject. "So, tell me, what do you think of Johnny's place?"

"It's fantastic." Kara suppressed a grin as she caught Bric's eye.

"Isn't it, though! Johnny and Dad did all the work. You should have seen it before they started renovations. Isn't that Lincoln bedroom something else?"

Kara almost choked on her coffee. She could feel herself blush from the top of her head to the tip of her toes and hoped Pam would attribute the color to her coughing fit.

Pam hurried to offer her a glass of water while Bric looked on, more amused than concerned. Kara wondered if his sister read the urge-to-kill look she shot him.

Assured that Kara was fine, Pam rushed blithely on, hardly pausing for breath. "What Dad doesn't know about woodworking and period furniture, Johnny does."

"Wouldn't my sister make a wonderful public relations director?"

Pam made a face at him. "Well, you never give yourself enough credit, so somebody has to." In another abrupt shift, she suggested to Kara, "How about a chocolate-chip cookie? They're *my* specialty."

At that moment the phone rang. Kara was grateful for the interruption. She needed a few moments to collect herself after that embarrassing sputter with the coffee. She found it difficult to follow Pam and sort out her own thoughts at the same time.

"For you," Pam said, holding out the receiver to her brother. "I was sure it was one of my teenagers with an earth-shattering crisis. Like no clean pair of jeans in the house.''

Bric pushed back his chair. "I'll take it in the study." On his way to the door, he inclined his head toward the baby. "Lynn's half-asleep. Maybe Kara would like to take her upstairs for a nap."

"Did Bric tell you about the cradle?" Pam asked as Kara followed her up the steps. "Dad made it for us kids, and we've already passed it around for the second generation. As the youngest, Johnny got it last." She paused, sighing almost wistfully. "Doesn't he have the perfect house to show it off? The truth is, though, he shuts up all but a few rooms when he's here alone. Sometimes the place seems more like a museum than a home."

Pam opened a door to another room, this one with a canopied bed covered by an embroidered quilt. Beside it stood a slatted walnut cradle, suspended from two high T-supports.

On the surface, Pam's commentary appeared offhand, but something in her voice told Kara that she knew about her brother's inability to have children. Knew it and, because of her affection for him, was unable to dismiss it.

She tucked Lynn into the small bed and began to swing the cradle gently to and fro.

"You won't have to worry about my hearing her when she wakes up," Pam assured Kara as they watched the infant's eyes drift shut. "I'll flip on the intercom system and catch the first peep she makes.

Lynn's a remarkably adjustable child, isn't she? Settled right into that bed without so much as a whimper."

"Sometimes she frets in unfamiliar surroundings, but she gets a lot of attention on the island. So she's learned to feel secure with different people. Then, too, the baby-sitter takes Lynn to her home every once in a while. I haven't been the only one caring for her."

"Still, it can't be easy for you. A single parent and all. Johnny says you lost your husband before Lynn was born. That's too bad." Pam laid a sympathetic hand on her shoulder.

Kara's body tensed. That was one misconception she should have cleared up long ago, but she could hardly tell Pam before she told Bric. "A lot of wonderful people have helped," she hedged. "Including your brother. He flew me to the hospital, you know, and waited until Lynn was born."

Pam walked over to sit on the edge of the bed. "You're in love with him, aren't you?"

Startled by the older woman's bluntness, Kara looked up and saw a familiar tenderness in Pam's warm brown eyes. So like her brother's, she mused. "Yes."

"And he's crazy about you. Can't stop talking about you or drag his eyes away from you. I must say I don't blame him. You're a beautiful woman."

Kara flushed at the compliment. "Thank you, but that's only because Bric makes me feel . . . special."

"If I were younger, I think I'd be terribly jealous." Pam laughed. "Of all my brothers and sisters, Johnny's my favorite. Since I'm twelve years older, I looked after him—like a second mother. I know Johnny very well, and it isn't easy for him to trust a woman. I guess you know he's been burned more than once."

"You mean Elaine and Gloria?"

"Exactly. I can't say I had much sympathy for Elaine. An iron maiden if there ever was one. She wasn't about to let anything stand in the way of her law degree. Well, she got what she wanted, but Johnny's built up a successful business without a college education. As far as that goes he's probably read more books than she has vocabulary.

"Now Gloria's a different story. More the Earth Mother type. But she up and dumped Johnny like he'd committed a crime or something. For a while I wasn't sure he was going to pull out of that one. Gloria's rejection really threw him for a loop."

"Then one day he bought this big old house and started turning it into a showplace. At the time I wondered if he wasn't trying to spite Gloria. Or maybe himself. All the same, it was great therapy. Not that he's worked the whole business out of his system yet. What Elaine and Gloria did—it warped him."

Pam smiled uncertainly. "I don't know what Johnny's told you. I don't even know if he realizes Gloria talked to me about the breakup. He claimed it was because the war had changed him." She paused. "I better shut my big mouth. I've said too much already."

Kara turned to lay a hand on Pam's arm. "Don't worry. You're not telling me something I don't know. Bric explained that he can't have children."

"I thought as much. It's not like Johnny to hide anything. But he's never mentioned it to the family. Male pride, I guess. Then when he did confide in someone, look what happened. With a clan like mine, I could certainly understand Gloria's desire for a family, but she handled the whole thing wrong. She really cared for Johnny, and it angered her when she couldn't have him and children, too. I think she was sorry later for some of the hurtful things she said. But enough of that." Pam eyed her companion speculatively. "Mind if I ask how you feel about Johnny's problem?"

By all rights, the question should have offended Kara, but she understood that Pam's brashness stemmed more from a love for Bric than a desire to meddle. "I'm not sure. I've always dreamed of having a big family. Maybe it's because I was an only child, but I think brothers and sisters are important."

"Obviously I have to agree." Her gaze drifted to Lynn. "There's nothing quite like having a baby, is there? Holding that new life in your arms. Still, these days there are alternatives." Pam shrugged. "Now I am getting too personal, even for me. Some things a woman—" She broke off as Bric walked in, wolfing down one of her cookies. "That was a short call," she noted lightly.

"Carlisle. We're having some trouble with one of the cargo planes, and he wanted to keep me posted." He came over and draped an arm around Kara's shoulder. "It's time we got ready for our day on the town."

Kara looked from Lynn to Pam. "Are you sure you don't mind staying here with the baby?"

"Mind? You have no idea of the chaos at my house." Pam chuckled. "Think of it! Here I can watch whatever TV shows I want without someone switching the channel on me."

"Don't be so sure. If Lynn wakes up hungry, she's apt to set up quite a squall. Then you won't think it's so peaceful."

"For me, handling one child is going to be a snap. There was a time I had to juggle half a dozen at once, and they don't necessarily get less demanding with age. But as a teacher, you know how that is." She got up and went to the door. "If you need anything, let me know. Bathroom's right through there."

"Thanks, Pam. It's been ages since I've had a whole day free."

"Don't mention it."

Before their tour, Kara excused herself to freshen up. After pulling on a warm sweater and ankle-high boots, she stood in front of a full-length mirror at the far end of the guest room to brush her long hair. This morning her talk with Pam had stirred up concerns she could no longer shove to a dark corner of her mind.

Kara worried her lower lip. The memory of her first meeting with Bric came flooding back, and she recalled how she'd unwittingly given him the wrong impression about Edmund. At the time it hadn't seemed to matter whether or not she set the record straight. After all, she hadn't envisioned falling in love with the man. Besides, she'd further reasoned, why cause herself added pain by dredging up the past?

Only later had Kara come to realize her mistake. Still she'd held her tongue—partly because she was embarrassed not to have been up-front from the start, partly because she feared Bric would think less of her. Trouble was, the longer she'd put off telling him, the easier it had been to delay the moment of truth.

But Pam's references to Elaine and Gloria had been a sharp reminder of her own deception. Bric's sister had made it clear that he was slow to trust. And for good reason. What, then, would he think when he learned she was not a widow?

All at once a cruel scenario played itself out in the mirror. She could almost picture herself remarking offhandedly, "Oh, by the way, Bric darling, my husband isn't dead. He's very much alive. I just thought you'd like to know."

Surely it wasn't too late to make Bric understand she hadn't deliberately set out to deceive him. Kara took a deep breath. She'd have to find the courage, as well as the right moment. And it had to be this weekend. No more delays.

Kara heard the bedroom door click shut seconds before Bric's image appeared in the cheval glass. He looked so handsome, so wonderful, and she loved him so desperately that she hated being the one to cause him pain. How would she bear it if her foolishness destroyed what they had together?

Bric capped her shoulders with his hands. "About ready?"

Kara twisted her head around, then guiltily turned it back, but her eyes found his in the glass. "Almost," she said, not quite able to make her feet move.

"Like your room?" His hand ran under the heavy fall of her hair and draped it over a shoulder.

"Yes, very much."

"Well," he murmured, stroking his fingers against the curve of her neck, "take a good look around. This's the last you're going to see of it for a while." He kept his eyes on her reflection. "As soon as Pam's on her way tonight, you're moving into mine."

"Is that so?" Bric didn't seem to notice that her voice sounded a little rehearsed or that she didn't quite return his gaze.

"Got a problem with that?" Sliding his hands down to her waist, he turned her in his arms.

"No," she answered hoarsely.

Then his mouth was on hers. Hot. Urgent. Demanding. Kara felt her knees go weak and her legs quiver. She clutched at his shirt to keep from sinking to the floor.

At last Bric lifted his head and smiled. "Until later," he promised.

Chapter Ten

The late-March weather couldn't have been more cooperative. It was a crisp but bright and sunny day, ideal for sightseeing.

Bric took Kara down to the harbor, where ice ridges, folded on the beach like a giant accordion, were already beginning to separate and thaw. He pointed to the small vessels, mounted on dry cradles along the shore, and the ships stranded in the frozen water. "Hard to believe, isn't it, that in less than four weeks this place'll be crawling with activity."

"What kind of boats use the bay?" Kara asked.

"Freighters, coal barges, ferry boats, tankers. You name it. If it floats, you'll see it in Sandusky Harbor at one time or another."

Before the morning was over, Bric and Kara sought out Follett House, a Greek revival mansion displaying Civil War relics. To their disappointment, the museum was still closed for the season. Although they walked around the building and peeked through the windows, they could see very little.

After stopping in a downtown café to warm up with hot coffee and a light lunch, they drove over the causeway to Johnson's Island where Confederate officers had once been imprisoned. Those who hadn't survived the war were buried in the northeast corner of the little island. Hand in hand they ambled around the small cemetery, reading the worn stone markers and wondering about the men who lay beneath them.

Kara was saddened by how young some of the soldiers had been. Peering at one of the graves of a lone Ohioan, she remarked, "How many, do you suppose, left wives and children behind? Or, more depressing, how many might have fathered sons or daughters they never even met? Maybe never even knew about."

Kara shuddered as the thought caused a guilty tightening in her chest. She renewed her resolve to make sure Edmund met Lynn.

Bric's arm came around her shoulder. "Cold?"

"A bit," she returned, knowing full well her trembling had little to do with the chill in the air.

"Time to thaw out again. And I know just the place. Sandusky Mall."

At the shopping center, Bric dragged Kara into a department store and headed straight for the toy section, where he made a great to-do about inspecting all the stuffed animals. After spending an inordinate amount of time debating between a shaggy dog and a teddy bear, he finally settled on an Easter bunny.

"For Lynn," he announced, handing it to Kara. "Now let's look at baskets."

"Baskets?"

"For my youngest nieces and nephews. While we're at it, we might as well put together some for the kids in your class."

By the time they were in the checkout line, they'd filled nine colorful wicker containers, each holding a special toy. In Sam and Delia's, they'd wedged among the candy eggs a family of floating ducks. "Can't forget the baby-to-be," Bric had proclaimed.

At the last minute, when Kara was loaded down with packages, Bric caught her off guard. From a display by the cash register, he pulled a helium balloon that broadcast You're Special. Attaching it to her wrist, he drawled, "My sentiments exactly." Kara's cheeks flushed a scalding red when the salesgirl tossed her a sly, knowing wink.

By chance, they ended the afternoon at the roller rink. They were stopped at a red light when a teenager, sporting a pair of skates around her neck, crossed in front of them and headed toward a large metal building.

"Now there's something I used to be pretty good at." Bric chuckled as he pointed at the shapely young blonde.

"I'll just bet you were," Kara observed dryly, deliberately mistaking his meaning.

Bric arched a brow. "Do I detect a note of jealousy?"

Sniffing loftily, Kara chided him, "Vanity isn't attractive. Besides—" She was on the verge of adding that he was old enough to be the girl's father, but she clamped down on the words. Though it was the standard comeback in these situations, it would have cut Bric deeply had she not caught herself in time.

"Besides what?"

"I'm not so bad on skates myself. Want to give the rink a whirl?"

"You're on."

At the counter Bric rented skates for them, and after taking several clumsy trial spins around the floor, they got the knack of staying upright.

Kara couldn't stifle a giggle at Bric's startled expression when his attempt to skate backward landed him on his rear. "Show-off," she taunted him as she sailed past and executed a neat turn. Seconds later a pint-size candidate for the roller derby came barreling down on her. When she attempted to swerve out of the way, her skates skidded from under her.

The spill sent both Kara and Bric into another burst of laughter.

A half hour later, Kara called time-out. "My class would love this place," she enthused as they glided toward the refreshment stand. "We haven't taken a field trip since early last fall. I wonder if I could sell the board on substituting an afternoon at the rink for a week's phys ed classes." She angled Bric a speculative glance. "Maybe they'd go for it if I threw in a tour of the museum and cemetery."

"Terrific idea. Need a chaperon?"

"Are you volunteering?"

"Why not?"

"I don't like to mention it, but what kind of chaperon spends as much time on his seat as on his feet?"

"What do you mean? I only fell four times." Bric dismissed the criticism with feigned offense. "Anyway, I haven't been on skates since I was ten. What's your excuse?"

"I don't need one. I'm the teacher."

"Cute!" he charged, giving her a playful cuff on the chin.

After finishing their large soft drinks, Bric asked, "Ready to go home?"

"Back to Perry's? Don't tell me you're bored with my company already," she teased him. "And here I thought I'd been invited to spend the night."

Bric guided them into a dimly lighted corner, where he pulled Kara into his arms. "I believe that tongue of yours is asking for another lesson."

"In that case—"

She didn't finish. Bric's mouth came down on hers with such force that it made her spin. The sensual assault didn't stop until her breath was coming quickly, erratically.

By the time he lifted his head, she could barely stand. "I love your brand of instruction," she murmured close to his lips.

"School's not out yet." Bric's mouth again took hers. This time the kiss was even more heated, more insistent. It was filled with all the desire that had been mounting in him since morning. Would he never get enough of her? he wondered.

Bric heaved a sigh and stood apart from her. "Better put an end to this lesson. Before I embarrass us both."

In Bric's study, Kara leaned back in the overstuffed chair and sipped at her sweet, minty cordial. Tonight she floated on a sea of contentment. That evening Bric had taken her to an elegant harbor restaurant, where they'd watched the fog roll in.

While he took a phone call in another room, Kara let her gaze roam the shelves along one wall. Obviously Bric's tastes were catholic. Hemingway, Bellow and Updike rubbed elbows with Robert Ludlum, Dick Francis and Ken Follett, while volumes of history, biography and poetry stood alongside texts on psychology, flying and woodworking.

She kicked off her shoes and strolled over to take a closer look at the framed document hanging above

Bric's desk. What from a distance had looked like some sort of certificate was actually a letter dated October 3, 1863. Kara guessed it must have been written by Bric's great-grandfather, who, he'd told her, had been a Yankee soldier. The letter served as yet another reminder of family, of roots. As if on this day she needed any more, she reflected ruefully.

Kara again sank into the chair. Her stockinged feet folded under her, she waited for Bric to return. After a time she let her eyes close, rested her head against the plump cushions and gave herself to the concerto playing softly in the background. Mozart. How fitting, she thought, a smile creeping over her lips.

Having grown up with a professor father and a lawyer mother, Kara appreciated the learning she found in others. It hadn't taken her long to realize that Bric was an educated man. Largely self-educated, but that only increased her admiration.

He was also a polished escort—as at home in the four-star restaurant where they'd had dinner as he'd been earlier in the small café where they'd eaten lunch. Beneath that veneer of worldliness, though, was a tenderness she hadn't expected when they first met. In jeans and leather flight jacket, he had come across all-confident, all-aggressive male. Not that she hadn't been immediately attracted by his aura of solidity. But it was the gentle man beneath who had won her heart.

Kara felt closer to Bric than she ever had to Edmund. No doubt because he was so straightforward. If only she could bring herself to be equally candid about her marital status. This afternoon she'd had the perfect opportunity, but because they'd never shared a wholly carefree day together, she'd been reluctant to let anything mar their pleasure. Still, she couldn't put off telling him much longer. Before tomorrow night, for sure.

At the sound of Bric's footsteps, Kara opened her eyes. When he passed through the open doorway, her pulse gave an excited leap. All thought of Edmund fled as Kara knew an immediate rush of desire.

Bric watched her eyes darken and momentarily froze in his tracks. Would there ever be a time when looking at her didn't rob him of breath? "Sorry if I startled you."

Kara noticed that his voice was a bit unsteady. She drew herself up as he walked toward her. "I must have drifted off for a minute."

Bric sat on the edge of the chair and trailed the back of one hand down her cheek. "You sure you're all right?"

"Positive. But how about you? A problem at the airport?"

He shrugged. "Routine. Our morning flights may have to be canceled because of the fog. Which means some heavy rescheduling, but it looks like everything'll work out. We won't be disturbed again." He took her glass and set it aside.

"If we are, I should have no trouble entertaining myself. I'm curious. Have you really read all these?" She indicated the books.

"Only once."

At his crooked smile, her heart did a flip-flop. "Too bad. I'd hoped you'd woo me by quoting Shakespeare or Keats."

"I have a much better idea." His lips coasted over hers in a leisurely kiss. "Mmm, you taste of crème de menthe. Intoxicating."

Instantly caught up in his embrace, Kara linked her hands around his neck. How was it he could make her forget everything with only the lightest of kisses?

Bric ran his hands over the silky material of her dress, his thumbs grazing the sides of her breasts. Soft. Warm. Feminine. And incredibly arousing. At her moan, a stab of need shot through him. It took all his willpower to dampen it. Tonight he was going to take it slow and easy. Tonight was for Kara. As he imagined arousing every inch of her sweet body, his hands came under her thighs and swept her into his arms.

"This is getting to be a habit," she murmured when he started for the door.

"A very good habit, wouldn't you agree?"

"One definitely worth cultivating."

In no time his long legs had cut through the living room and neared the stairs. "I hope Sunshine likes her new bed. What I have in mind is going to take the better part of the night."

Kara touched her temple to his as he strode up the steps and down the hall. "We should check on her first, Bric. See if she's all right."

"I just did. And the intercom's on."

"Do you always plan this well?"

He bumped a hip against the bedroom door and shouldered his way through. "Only when something's very important. Like you. Like tonight." He kissed her as he gently laid her on the bed and came down beside her.

"Oh, Bric," Kara whispered. "It's been such a perfect day."

"Has it, darling? For me, too, but it's not over yet."

"I wish . . . I wish it could be like this forever."

"There's no reason it can't."

Her fingers shook as she traced the shape of his mouth. "Nothing lasts forever."

"Oh, no?" he drawled raggedly. "Let's see how long we can make this last." Lifting his fingers, he kissed each soft tip, then bent and rubbed his mouth over hers.

With sensuous slowness, he outlined the contours of her lips. Sipping and teasing, his tongue cruised the sensitive centerline. On a small, throaty sound, she opened to him.

The kiss was wide and warm and ardent. Kara cradled the back of his neck and pressed him closer. She was aware only of the movement of his lips over hers, the lazy exploration of his tongue, which invited a reciprocal boldness.

His mouth lingered on hers until Kara was weak with longing. She knew nothing except that she wanted to be brought together with this man who had taught her the meaning of passion, the meaning of love. His hands roved her body as his lips rolled and rocked over hers. She clutched his shoulders and gave herself up to the flood of sensations overwhelming her.

Bric's mouth idled over her chin and down her neck. Desperately he clung to a shred of restraint. While his tongue bathed the sensitive hollow, one hand tilted her toward him; the other unzipped her slinky black dress and eased it off.

Fingers trembling, Kara released the buttons of Bric's shirt and slid her hands beneath the parted fabric to splay across his chest.

"I've got to have you," he groaned, his mouth tracking the fragile lace that rode above the slope of her breasts.

"Then take me," she breathed in a shaky whisper.

"Not yet, love." He lowered his lips over the flimsy material and drew the hardened peak into his mouth. As he suckled languidly, his hands moved to her undergarments. One by one they fell away.

When he lightly raked his nails down her bare flesh, from collarbone to breastbone to hip and back again, Kara quivered. Pushing the broadcloth shirt from his shoulders, she rubbed herself against him, urging him to cover her nakedness with his.

"Oh, sweetheart," he growled. "I can't last much longer if you do that."

"Let me see you, Bric. All of you." She ran her hands beneath his belt, then located his zipper.

"Careful, love," he said, tensing his stomach muscles. "We have to respect the equipment, imperfect though it is."

"I hadn't noticed any flaws." She smiled as he stripped away their remaining clothes.

Kara thought Bric had taught her all there was to know about loving, but she was wrong. With caressing hands and mouth, he led her from one peak to another, each higher than the last. Finally she could wait no more for the union her body demanded. Together they found an explosive fulfillment that left them drained and entwined in each other's arms.

Kara awoke to soft burbling sounds mingled with a low-pitched masculine whisper. It took her a few seconds to remember where she was and identify the voices.

In the next room Bric was changing Lynn. His fingers, which had no trouble wielding a hammer or soldering delicate wires, fumbled with the closure on the disposable diaper. But then wood and metal didn't squirm, he consoled himself. "Hold still, now, Merry Sunshine," he told the wiggling baby. "We don't want to wake up your mother. She needs her sleep."

Lynn gave him a bubbly smile while he snapped her sleeper shut and folded the covers under her chin.

Wrapped in a dressing gown, Kara stopped in the doorway to observe the domestic scene. Bric had thrown on a robe that came no farther than mid-thigh. Beneath the terry, his bare legs protruded at an awkward angle as he crouched over Lynn.

After last night, Kara had thought it impossible to love him more. But right now her heart overflowed with emotion.

Swaying the cradle, he cajoled quietly, "Close those big blue eyes now. It's not morning yet. Your mother and I have some unfinished business."

"We do, do we?"

Bric turned and caught Kara in the warm glow of the night-light. He saw that her mouth was still softly swollen from his kisses. Her hair framed her face in appealing disarray. "Come here, woman."

"You need help?" she inquired, knowing that was not at all what was on his mind.

"I need *you*." Grabbing a hand, he towed her to him and kissed her long and hard.

"You do wild things to my senses," he breathed into her hair.

"Funny. You have the same effect on me."

"Then we ought to do something about it."

"You're insatiable." Kara smiled, pleased that she could arouse him just by being herself.

"That's why we should make this arrangement permanent." He tipped up her chin and looked deeply into her eyes. "Marry me, Kara. Let me be a husband to you, a father to Lynn."

For an endless span of minutes, she didn't speak. Tears welled behind her lids. She had to tell him about her past. And she had to do it now, before she lost her nerve.

"Bric," she began, "there's something I need to explain . . . about my husband."

Bric took Kara's face into his hands and riveted her gaze with his. "I'm going to make you forget there was ever any man before me. I'm going to fill your mind. Fill you. Completely."

With the pads of his thumbs, he lazily etched crescents beneath her eyes, then lowered his head and sealed her mouth in a kiss that drove out all but the here, the now.

Chapter Eleven

Kara didn't know that it was possible to be so happy and at the same time so miserable. When she'd first given herself to Bric, she'd only wanted to confirm her love. It had been enough, she'd reasoned, to be together, to be close.

Now as she lay quietly beside him, she worried that when he woke he would press her for a wedding date. Last night she hadn't definitely accepted his proposal, nor had she flatly turned it down. In the end, a renewed burst of passion had saved her from any reply at all.

Why, she wondered, did a small part of her persist in holding back? Did she fear she would come to regret Bric's inability to give her children? No, she conceded, not anymore. Her feelings for him were the most intense she'd ever known, and Kara didn't like to imagine how empty life would be if they should part. Exactly when Bric's sterility had ceased to be an issue, she couldn't say, but during the past months her priorities had experienced a subtle shift, and the flesh-and-blood man had become far more important to her than a large family.

Besides, as for having other babies, weren't there the alternatives Pam had mentioned? Every day modern medicine seemed to perform new miracles. Maybe there would be one for them. If not, so be it.

Though Kara no longer harbored any doubts that she and Bric could build a happy future, this morning she'd awakened to another, graver concern. She feared his reaction when he learned she wasn't the bereft widow he'd imagined. As long as he didn't know the truth, she could hold on to what they had. But she expected that he'd be unforgiving once she confessed to dodging the facts—no matter what the reason. A man who'd misplaced his trust in women twice before was not going to look upon the third time as a charm.

Rolling onto her side, Kara curled into a tight ball. Was that why she'd been dragging her feet? It wasn't as if he'd never tried to broach the subject. Yet whenever she'd been on the verge of bringing it up, something else had intervened.

But last night time had run out.

Kara felt Bric stir beside her. Seconds later his arm circled her waist and nudged her close. "Good morning," he whispered.

"Good morning," she returned, unable to resist snuggling against his comforting warmth. Even as she curved into his body, her mind shouted, *Tell him now! He loves you. He'll understand.*

Twisting to face him, she brought a hand to his shoulder and smiled weakly. "Bric, before we set a wedding date, there's something I need to say."

"You already did, sweetheart. That kiss was a yes, wasn't it?"

Not ready to meet his eyes, Kara pressed her forehead to his chest. "It was a yes. But we've got to talk."

Just then a plaintive cry from Lynn commanded Bric's attention. Bolting upright, he leaped from bed and began to pull on his robe. "Later, love. There's plenty of time to work out all the wedding details. Right now, Sunshine needs us."

Kara didn't know whether to be relieved or frustrated. Sighing, she felt for her dressing gown at the foot of the bed. "It's probably the strange room."

She was working one arm into a sleeve when Bric leaned over and pinned her to the mattress. He took time to kiss her soundly, then suggested, "Let me take care of this. You stay here. I'll get Lynn's bottle and bring her into our bed. Then—" he beamed engagingly "—together we'll tell her the good news."

Bric was so incredibly sweet and the baby so blissfully content cuddled between them that talking about

Edmund was out of the question. The moment was too perfect, too precious, to risk ruining. There would be another chance later today, she told herself.

But shortly after a late brunch, Carlisle called from the hangar. One of the mechanics had taken ill, leaving them shorthanded. And now that the fog had begun to lift, the crew was swamped.

Reluctantly Bric flew Kara and Lynn home sooner than he'd planned. There was time for only a hasty parting on her doorstep, but he promised to drop by the next day if he could get away. Or for sure on Tuesday.

Running his thumb over her lips, he lamented, "I may have to take an hour or so to help Joey again. Do you mind terribly?"

"You should know me better than to ask."

He kissed her once more, the tenderness of his lips thanking her more eloquently than any words. "I know it's weeks yet before Edith's birthday, but Joey's not going to let me rest until that present is finished, neatly wrapped and tied with a bow." His mouth touched hers one last time before he loped down the walk toward the airport pickup.

It was almost four o'clock on Monday, and Kara was about to dig in to a stack of homework papers when she heard a familiar squeak of brakes. Bric! He'd made it today, after all!

Jumping up, she hurried to the window and drew aside the drape. Sure enough, his dilapidated pickup was parked out front. Strange, though, he wasn't alone. She could definitely make out the profile of someone in the passenger seat. Could it be the elusive Mark Carlisle? Kara had met the man only once. Last weekend when she'd expressed an interest in getting to know him better, Bric had teasingly threatened to keep her away from the dashing bachelor until they were safely married.

Curious, Kara cocked her head as Bric leaped from the truck. Even at a distance she sensed a bridled agitation in the rigid set of his body. Goodness, was he really worried that she might be attracted to his best friend? Partly flattered, partly amused, she blinked into the glare of sunlight glinting off the windowpane.

As Bric and the other man neared the front walk, panic welled in her throat, nearly cutting off her air. It was no stranger who accompanied Bric to her door.

It was Edmund.

How many months had it been since she'd seen him? Ten? Eleven? Though Kara's heart thumped madly against her rib cage, a strange numbness held her immobile. As she watched the two men come toward her, she recalled every detail from that day Edmund had walked out of her life.

The morning started with a visit to her doctor. Only after Kara arrived home did the full impact of his report hit her. Flinging her arms wide, she executed a neat pirouette and shouted for joy. She was pregnant! At long last she was pregnant!

To Kara, it hardly seemed possible. Edmund had never been particularly demonstrative. Not even during the early days of their marriage. On those occasions when they had made love, he'd invariably rushed to a hurried consummation that had left her unfulfilled . . . and feeling inadequate as a woman.

When after months of frustration, she'd finally worked up the nerve to broach the subject, Edmund had lashed out at her. Wasn't she satisfied that he was busting his butt to get ahead, to make her proud? Didn't she realize that working for his mother-in-law placed an extra burden on him, that he had to be twice as good as the next guy to prove he wasn't getting a free ride? Couldn't she tell that he was just too damned tired to play Don Juan?

Kara had come away from their confrontation feeling selfish and unappreciative. Trying to look at the situation from Edmund's point of view, she'd made up her mind to exercise more patience. Their relationship was bound to improve as soon as he was well established in his career.

But it hadn't.

By the final year of their marriage she and Edmund had been intimate so seldom that Kara could name the very night Lynn had been conceived.

As was his habit, Edmund had arrived home quite late. Though Kara had turned in early, sleep had eluded her. At her touch he'd flopped onto his side, but she'd swallowed her pride and taken the initiative. She'd eventually warmed him to her, but their union had been as disappointing as ever.

Now, two months after that degrading episode, she found herself pregnant.

Kara's fingers shook with excitement as she dialed Edmund's office. When at last she got through, she urged him to come home early. "For a surprise," she hinted, certain the baby would bring to them the closeness she craved. "It's Saturday, dear. You don't have to burn the midnight oil again, do you?"

No sooner had she gotten out the request than Edmund halted her cheerful flow of words. "Okay, okay, but don't expect me before seven-thirty."

Though she detected a curious edge to his voice, Kara refused to let it dim her high spirits. She spent the rest of the day planning a romantic dinner for two, which included a drive across town to pick up a bottle of Edmund's favorite champagne. It was already icing when she heard his key turn in the front lock.

At the door, Kara twisted her arms about her husband's neck and awarded him with an especially affectionate welcome. "Dinner's about ready, but first I have the most—"

Before she could utter another syllable, he pried himself from her embrace and took a step backward. "Hold on, Kara. Give me a minute to wind down, will you?"

Though the rebuff wounded, she was more stricken by the troubled look darkening Edmund's face. "What is

Without answering, he led her to the sofa. "I've got to get something off my chest."

She sat beside him and drew her fingers down his cheek. "What's wrong? Have you lost an important case?"

"No," he said, avoiding her eyes. "As a matter of fact, my work couldn't be going better."

"Then why the gloomy expression?"

"It's a . . . personal problem."

"Personal? You're not ill, are you? Is it your heart? Maybe you ought to take some time off."

"No, I'm fine. I said personal, not physical. Personal," he repeated. "As in you and me."

"What about us?"

"I suppose there's no diplomatic way to put it. So I'll be blunt. I've found someone else."

"I'm afraid I don't understand."

"To tell the truth, neither do I. It just happened, that's all. One thing led to another, and...I'm sorry."

He droned on, but Kara pulled her back straight and tuned out his voice. She wasn't interested in feeble excuses for infidelity or false shows of regret. When Edmund identified the woman, she knew exactly why he wanted out of their marriage. She ached to shriek that he couldn't do this to her, that she was carrying his baby. But she was too grief-stricken to force out the protest. All she knew was that she never again wanted to set eyes on Edmund Reynolds.

* * *

And now here he was on his way up her front walk. His timing couldn't have been worse. But then timing, she reflected wryly, had never been Edmund's forte.

At the brisk knock, Kara let go of the breath she'd been holding. Her palms damp with moisture, she opened the door and found herself face-to-face with Bric's glower and Edmund's ingratiating smile. Though she tried to summon up a greeting, the words lodged in her throat.

"You look like you've seen a ghost," Bric charged mockingly. "But you can wipe that stricken expression off your face. The man beside me is very much alive." He swiveled brusquely on a heel and strode down the steps.

For several seconds Kara stood riveted to the spot, her gaze fastened on Bric's proud back. He was about to slam into the pickup when she finally roused herself and darted out the door. "Bric, wait! Don't go!" Before she got halfway down the walk, he'd taken off in a swirl of gravel.

The angry snarl of his truck reverberated on the still air as Kara doggedly retraced her steps. Why today, of all days, did her ex-husband have to show up? Hadn't he messed up her life enough as it was?

Her front door had barely clicked shut before she demanded, "How did you find me?"

Though a muscle twitched in Edmund's jaw, his tone was level. "No hello, Kara?" Slipping off his topcoat, he said, "Through my connections at the State Board of Education."

"By all means, make yourself at home." She was more angry at herself than at him. Why hadn't she told Bric everything last weekend?

Indifferent to her cold welcome, Edmund hung his tailored cashmere on the coat tree beside the entry. He took time to straighten his jacket and shoot his cuffs before claiming a chair. "When I got your address, I must admit to being somewhat flabbergasted. I never expected an island. Why, Kara? Why such a godforsaken place?"

"What would you have had me do, Edmund? Stay on in Cincinnati and drown in pity?" She sat down on the couch and watched him arrange the crease in his trousers. "Anyhow, I happen to like it here."

"Is that right? I can't believe your preferences include this tacky—*antiquated* is probably a kinder word—decor. It's hardly your style."

"Ultramodern was your taste, Edmund, not mine. I happen to find this apartment quite comfortable."

"To each his own." His glance traveled over the secondhand furnishings but stopped short at Lynn's playpen. "Good Lord. Do you run a nursery school, too?"

Shrugging off the question, Kara struggled to marshall some positive feelings for Edmund. Had she once been in love with this seeming stranger? Could he actually be the father of her child?

Though it was difficult for her to fathom, that was her ex-husband occupying the chair across from her. By rights she should lead him directly to Lynn. But first, she would learn what had prompted his unexpected visit. Eyeing him suspiciously, she probed, "What brings you here, Edmund?"

"Guilt. Pure and simple guilt."

Odd, Kara reflected, he should admit to the same moral burden that had been plaguing her for weeks. Could his remorse be attributed to an attack of scruples? Perhaps, but she knew better than to let down her guard. More than likely her ex-husband had some angle.

Folding a leg beneath her, she allowed, "Guilt is hardly pure and rarely simple."

"Maybe a poor choice of adjectives, but, Kara, you have to believe me when I say I feel damned rotten about what happened."

"It's a bit late for self-recriminations, isn't it?"

"Granted, but my conscience has been giving me hell. Even my work has suffered."

"If you're looking for sympathy, you've come to the wrong place."

"Not sympathy, Kara. Forgiveness."

"You traveled all this way to ask my forgiveness? Wouldn't a phone call have done as well?"

"I was afraid you wouldn't talk to me. It's important you understand. The thing between Monica and me... I've come to realize it was nothing but an attack of hormones."

"*Was?*"

"Yes, was." He got up and joined her on the couch, not objecting when she scooted to the far end. "Monica and I are through."

"Oh?"

"I made a dreadful mistake, darling," he insisted, failing to notice Kara's wince at the endearment. "Monica's not the woman I thought she was. She's no fun anymore. All she does is nag about having a baby."

"I suppose you've been putting her off the way you did me. What's the matter? Isn't she buying your the-time's-not-right argument?"

"Look, Kara, I've already filed for divorce. I had to. Her whining drives me up the wall. I'm too busy for children. Especially since I'm planning to run for the state legislature. If elected, I'll never have a free moment. Even you agreed that an absentee father's no kind of parent. But Monica won't listen to reason."

Kara could guess what lay behind Edmund's decision to leave his wife. Chances were it wasn't because Monica had been pressing him to start a family but because her father, who sat on the state supreme court, had recently been charged with bribery. No doubt Edmund saw the scandal as a threat to his political career.

Kara's eyes narrowed. "This breakup wouldn't have anything to do with Judge Lewis, would it?"

Edmund was aghast. "You mean you heard? Here?"

"Perry's Island isn't the end of the earth. We do get newspapers and television."

"I admit I'm disappointed in the judge. I had nothing but admiration for the man, and he let me down. But that's beside the point. I left Monica because I finally came to my senses. I want you back, darling. We were a dynamite team once, and we can be again. Think of us on the campaign trail! With you by my side, I can't lose."

"If you're after image, Edmund, Monica's perfect. She's beautiful, poised, articulate."

"Yes, but she's not you. I didn't appreciate what I had until after I lost you, Kara. But that doesn't mean we can't make a fresh start." He inched his way toward her. "Tell me you want that, too. Say you'll marry me again."

"You don't want a wife, Edmund. You want an asset. Surely you can find a woman better able to further your career. You did it before."

"Do you know how much it hurts me to hear you say that? How it pains me for you to believe I married Monica because of her father's political clout? I told you, it was chemistry."

"That's more than we had going for us."

"Oh, Kara," he said mournfully, "I realize we didn't make love as often as you'd have liked, but it wasn't from any lack of emotion on my part. If you must know, my feelings for you were above the carnal. I worshiped the ground you walked on. You're the only woman I've ever truly loved."

Kara had to hand it to her ex-husband. Edmund was so successful at pretense that he duped not only others but also himself. Each fabrication his mind concocted, he believed to be the truth. She'd once mistaken that veneer of sincerity for charm. But no more.

"I suppose I should be flattered," Kara remarked, "but if I was on a pedestal when we were married, I think you should know I didn't appreciate the view. Face it, Edmund. It's too late for us. But that doesn't mean we can't be friends."

"I think not. If you're unwilling to commit yourself to my team," he carped peevishly, "what's the purpose?"

She stood up. "If you need a reason, there's a very good one behind that closed door. It's about time you two were introduced." With that, Kara guided him to the bedroom and snapped on a table lamp beside Lynn's crib.

"A baby? Are you sitting for someone?"

"Not at all. She's mine. Meet Lynn."

"*Yours?* How can that be?" His eyes became two slits as he studied Kara more closely. "You're not having a little fun at my expense, are you?" When she didn't reply, he went on, "Well, this is a surprise, all right. I suppose that hulk in the aviator jacket's the father. That would explain the little scene I witnessed when he dropped me off. I must say I never figured you for such a fast worker, my dear." Frowning, he looked back at the sleeping infant.

All of a sudden he whipped around, his fists angrily balled at his sides. "Why, she's no newborn. Tell me, who were you running around with behind my back?"

Though livid, outwardly Kara remained impassive. She wondered if Edmund saw the irony in his accusation. It was all right for him to cheat on her, but heaven forbid she should turn the tables. In a controlled voice she warned him, "Is that any way to talk in front of your daughter?"

"To think, I was torturing myself, worried sick that I'd wronged you when all along—" He stopped in midsentence, his brow wrinkling. "What did you say?"

"I suggested you mind your manners."

"No, the other. What did you call this baby?"

"Your daughter."

"You expect me to believe this child is mine? She can't be."

"I'm not surprised you're skeptical. But I did manage to climb off my pedestal on a few occasions. Or were they so forgettable that you don't remember?"

"That's unfair, Kara."

"Don't talk to me about fair! Remember the night you moved out? We never did get around to my surprise. Well, here she is."

"You're serious, aren't you?" Backing away, Edmund combed manicured fingers through his hair. "You're sure there's no mistake?"

"Whatever you may think, I was a faithful wife, Edmund. Lynn can't be another man's child. There was no other man."

He cleared his throat. "I see. Well, this is... It's unexpected."

Kara waited while he collected himself, but she had to make an effort not to smile. It was a novel sight to see Edmund rattled. To help them both over the awkwardness, she invited, "Wouldn't you like a closer look? Come over here. She's beginning to wake up."

Cautiously he approached the crib and placed both hands on the railing. "She is kind of cute. What did you say you call her?"

"Lynn." Lifting the baby into her arms, Kara asked, "Would you like to hold her?"

Edmund extended a defensive palm. "Let's not rush things. Give me time to get used to the idea of being a father."

"Okay, but I guarantee she'll grow on you. Lynn's such a joy, Edmund. I'll bring her to see you whenever you like. I owe you that."

"You mean have her visit me? Good grief, Kara. What in the world would I do with her?"

"Love her. Play with her. Get to know what she likes and doesn't like. All the things a parent does."

"Let's not get carried away here. I'm not much good with babies. We'd better put the visits on hold. For the time being, anyhow. Maybe when she's older we can get acquainted."

Incredulous, Kara hugged Lynn close. "You mean you don't care if you see her or not?"

"I didn't say that. Sure I'd like to see her from time to time. But don't expect me to keep her over weekends or for holidays or summers. As for child support, I can't promise much. My divorce is going to set me back a pretty penny. Monica's out for my hide. Then there's the campaign..."

"Don't give it a second thought," Kara said stiffly. "We're getting along fine."

"I intend to do my share, of course. Later, when things ease up, I'll send you something." Thoughtfully he rubbed his chin. "It's too bad, really, we won't all be together. I bet she's damned photogenic. You know, a newspaper picture or two wouldn't hurt my campaign."

Kara set her lips in a tight line. "Don't even think of it! Lynn's no political pawn."

"I was afraid you wouldn't go for that. Can't blame me for trying." He rubbed his hands together. "Well, I'd better be going."

Blinking back tears, Kara watched her ex-husband stride toward the door. She should be hurt. She should be angry. But all she felt was pity. It broke her heart to think Edmund was going to miss out on all the joy of watching Lynn grow up. How pathetic that he was too self-absorbed to care!

In contrast, Kara thought of Bric.

As Edmund pulled on his expensive topcoat, his eyes drifted one last time over the apartment. "What a waste...your living here."

"I wouldn't expect you to understand. Shall I call for the airport pickup?"

"Don't bother. I'll walk."

After he'd left, a look of deep sadness crossed Kara's face. Edmund hadn't made a move to touch their daughter, let alone hold her. Nor had he bothered to ask the date of her birth.

The paper clip Bric had been twisting and untwisting broke with an abrupt snap. Flipping the jagged halves onto his desk, he cursed soundly. Women! They were all alike. Insincere, deceitful, conniving.

When the dissonance of the phone sliced into his tirade, he flinched. He could guess who was on the other end of the line. If he hadn't taken some sort of perverse pleasure in being reminded of what a sap he'd been, he'd have taken the phone off the hook hours ago. She'd been calling at five-minute intervals all afternoon and evening—ever since he'd returned to the office after flying her ex-husband back to Sandusky.

Her *ex*-husband. Bric nearly strangled on the word. Kara had pretended to be a widow when all along she'd been divorced. Not that he had anything against divorced women. What galled him was that her duplicity was a deliberate attempt to play on his sympathies.

Turning a deaf ear to the jangling phone, Bric propped his booted feet on the desk and meticulously inspected the scuffed toes. Damn her! Chump that he was, he'd fallen for that false air of innocence.

Moreover, she'd suckered not only him but her husband, as well. On the flight back to the mainland, Reynolds had confided that Lynn was a total surprise. What was Kara trying to pull? Why had she kept the baby a secret? To the man's credit, he'd seemed to take the news in his stride. If Bric had been in his place, he wouldn't have been so forgiving.

On the fifteenth ring, he shoved away from his desk. What he needed was a stiff drink. Snatching up his jacket, he tore out the door, hardly aware that the phone had at long last fallen silent.

Four hours later, Bric was still church sober, his senses not the least dulled to Kara's deception. He took the steps to his porch two at a time and jammed his key into the front lock. In his entryway, he flipped on the overhead light and shielded his eyes against the sudden glare.

Feeling defeated, Bric slogged toward his study and dropped onto the same overstuffed chair Kara had curled up in two short days ago. Wearily, he closed his eyes on the memory and struggled against a suffocating despair.

Had it only been that afternoon when he'd taken off on the routine flight to Perry's? At the same time, he couldn't help wondering what business his passenger had on the island. Something to do with the winery, he'd guessed. The man's polished manner suggested he might be a restaurateur interested in a new vintner.

The plane had barely left the ground when Bric had commented, "The Linskey label's gaining quite a reputation. As it well deserves. I expect you're wanting to check out what the winery has to offer."

"That's a tempting suggestion, but I doubt I'll have time."

"You're not here to test the wines for some restaurant?"

"Hardly. My errand's personal. By the way, I'm Edmund Reynolds."

"Hmm. That's the name of the schoolteacher on the island. You her...brother-in-law?"

Edmund had smiled. "No, her husband. Her ex, I should say."

Shock had knocked the breath out of Bric. Somehow he'd mumbled his own name by way of introduction, but a sharp drop of the Cessna had betrayed the jolt to his senses.

Throughout the remainder of the flight, he'd fought hard to maintain a calm exterior. It was no easy task when his insides were a seething caldron of emotions. Confusion, jealousy, fury, had filled his mind with dozens of unanswered questions. If at that instant he could have gotten his hands on Kara!...

In the darkness of his office, Bric sank deeper into the wide, soft-cushioned chair. After a time, his feverish mind was delivered to the blessed release of sleep.

All too soon the desk phone woke him. Automatically he hoisted himself up and grabbed the receiver.

"Hello," he grumbled thickly.

"Bric? Thank God!"

The sound of Kara's voice slapped him awake, but he had no words for her. A pithy silence hummed over the wire before she coaxed, "Bric? Are you there?"

He removed the receiver from his ear and suspended it for a few seconds above the phone. While his jaw clenched and unclenched, he slowly lowered his hand over the plunger.

In desperation, Bric propelled himself out of his chair and blundered toward the guest room. He would sleep there, he decided, since Kara's lingering scent in his own bed would stir up too many bittersweet memories. Groping his way in the dark, he sagged onto the mattress, twisted off his boots and plopped them on the floor. After pulling his shirt free of his pants, he fell back against the pillows.

But the sleep he sorely needed evaded him. All night long he nursed a crippling anger. By dawn he realized that he'd get no rest until he'd had it out with Kara. In a rush, he pulled his boots back on and, before he could talk himself out of it, was on his way to the hangar.

Some forty-five minutes later he stood pounding on Kara's door, prepared to reduce it to toothpicks if she didn't respond. When at last her footsteps sounded in the living room, he squared his shoulders and braced his feet in a wide stance.

"What is it?" Kara questioned as the door swung open. Wrapped in a long robe, she looked out at him from puffy, red-rimmed eyes.

It was all Bric could do to keep himself from hauling her into his arms. But hurt overrode the more tender feelings an openly vulnerable Kara inspired.

For a fraction of a second, Kara could have sworn he'd looked contrite. But with lightning swiftness the angles and planes of his face hardened into an accusing mask.

She took a long step backward, not wanting him to touch her, even accidentally, as he brushed past. Why had he bothered to come? And at such an hour of the morning! Hadn't his hanging up on her said it all?

Kara felt her spine straighten and her chin tilt derisively. She'd spent a sleepless night worrying about him, wondering how in the world she would ever make him understand. But his dark scowl told her she might as well save her breath. Obviously he'd come looking for a fight, not a reconciliation.

Well, if a fight was what he wanted, she'd give him his money's worth!

Kara sucked in her breath and let her temper fly. "Why did you cut me off like that when I phoned? Before you say one word," she spat out, "I know I should have told you about Edmund a long time ago. I tried. And I can't go back and change that. All I can do is—"

Bric finished for her. "Manufacture a few more lies."

A look of incredulity rounded Kara's eyes. "I have never willfully lied to you!"

"That's funny. I could have sworn you said your husband was dead."

The accusation hit its mark. "Please believe me, Bric, I didn't consciously set out to mislead you. Though I have to admit I sidestepped the issue, by no stretch of the imagination was I trying to be devious."

Bric's laugh was filled with mockery. "Telling me you'd *lost* your husband wasn't devious?"

Kara's mouth worked up and down, but no words came. She turned sad eyes on Bric. "I didn't mean that the way it sounded. You took it wrong."

"Yet you never bothered to straighten me out!"

"The time never seemed right!"

"In all these months you couldn't spare a few minutes for a little honesty?" The corners of his mouth dipped downward in a grimace. "I even told Pam your husband was dead. You must have had a real good laugh at the fools you made of us. About how sorry we were for you. A pregnant widow."

Kara gasped. So *that* was it, the source of Bric's feelings. He'd *pitied* her all along. He didn't love her. And why had he tacked on that bit about her pregnancy? Of course! How dense could one person be? Bric had made no secret of the fact he wanted children but couldn't have them. Yet here was poor, bereft Kara. The perfect opportunity for a ready-made family!

She'd been right to be cautious about getting involved with Bric. Too bad she hadn't followed her instincts. Kara leveled him a look that would have withered the devil himself. "I think you know what you can do with your pity."

"Pity? What's pity got to do with it?" His nostrils flared with rage.

"Quiet," Kara whispered. "You're going to wake the baby."

At the mention of Lynn, a stark desolation coursed through Bric. He didn't need a psychologist to point out how blindly jealous he was of Edmund Reynolds. And not only because of Kara. Bric couldn't name the moment he'd started thinking of Lynn as his own, but he had. The notion that her real father was alive and had a greater claim to her was almost more than he could bear.

Still, she was the man's flesh and blood. And Kara had robbed him of his rights as a father. Not the same way Bric himself had been cheated by Elaine, but close. With the sardonic lift of an eyebrow, he jeered, "How about keeping Lynn from Reynolds? Was she something else you never got around to revealing?"

"What?" Kara mumbled, thrown off balance by the unexpected question.

"Your ex-husband had quite a shock, didn't he? How could you have done that to him, Kara?"

"Oh, Bric, must you make snap judgments? Give me a chance to explain."

"Don't put yourself out. I've played this scene before. Different woman, but the script's familiar."

The note of disdain was shattering. Kara bit her lips, tears prickling the backs of her eyes, but she refused to give Bric the satisfaction of seeing her cry. She tilted her mouth scornfully. "If that's what you think, then you, sir, can take up residence in Hades."

On that final outburst, Kara dodged past Bric and jerked open the door.

"Thanks for the lesson, *Mrs.* Reynolds, but I'm well acquainted with the terms. As they say, women make the best teachers."

Chapter Twelve

Mrs. Reynolds, this Civil War stuff's boring," Billy complained as he slapped his book shut. "Why do we have to study history, anyway?"

"Because people learn from their mistakes. History teaches us how to avoid repeating them."

And if that was true, Kara chided herself, then she should have learned her lesson long ago: stay away from men.

She sat down at the desk next to Billy's. "I know reading about history can sometimes be pretty deadly, but there are ways of making it come alive. Not long ago I visited Follett House and Johnson's Island and felt as if I'd been transported back to Civil War times." Kara smiled. "I've been thinking, maybe we could take a field trip there before the school year ends.''

''How 'bout this Friday?'' Sam suggested.

''I thought you were supposed to be looking over *Macbeth* for that quiz I'm giving you next week.''

''Your conversation was more interesting.''

Kara shook her head. ''Friday's only three days away. I don't think we could make all the arrangements that fast.''

''Sure we could.''

''But there are so many details to take care of. Transportation to start with—''

''No sweat,'' Sam interrupted. ''My dad would be more than happy to lend us a winery man to get us to the airstrip. Then once we're in Sandusky, we could rent a set of wheels. Maybe a limo,'' he teased her.

''I can just see the board approving that expense,'' Kara said dryly.

Sam grinned. ''Can't blame a man for trying.''

As her students continued making plans, Kara couldn't help being carried away on the tide of their enthusiasm. On impulse she even suggested that they top off the trip by going to the skating rink.

Ruth's eyes rounded. ''Oh, could we? I've never been skating.''

''Boy, that would be fun,'' Joey said excitedly.

''I hate to be a spoil sport,'' Delia commented, ''but if you're going skating, I'd better beg off.''

''Why?'' Sam asked, surprised.

She pointed to her burgeoning stomach. "Don't want to take any chances at this stage in the game."

Though Sam tried his best to change her mind, Delia stood her ground. In the end he decided against going as well but did arrange for Kara to borrow one of the winery vans.

That Friday morning she picked up the children for the early flight to Sandusky. At Follett House the four were led through the museum by a guide. Then later, at Johnson's Island, Kara provided the historical details. Although they pretended interest, Kara knew exactly what was on their minds. When would they get through with all this school stuff and go skating?

Right after lunch, Kara pulled the rental car into a parking space alongside the rink. As she cut the engine, she looked directly at each of her students. "Now, listen up. I know none of you has been on skates before, so I want you take things easy. Your folks would have a fit if I brought you home all banged up. Okay?"

Kara should have known caution was asking too much of them. Still, their antics did have compensations. So occupied was she with telling Joey and Ruth not to do this and Billy and Ralph not to do that, that she almost forgot about Bric. Almost but not quite. Since she'd slammed the door in his face nearly a week ago, she'd tried hard to put him out of her mind. Yet he always seemed to be lurking somewhere around the edges.

The pain Kara endured that afternoon whenever he entered her thoughts was nothing compared with what she later suffered at Sandusky Airport. They were hurrying through the terminal to catch the five-twenty flight just as Bric walked out a door marked Erie Islands Air Service. At once Kara's heart plummeted to her stomach, then jumped to her throat.

Before she could stop him, Joey took off, shouting, "Mr. Brickner, Mr. Brickner."

Bric stooped to check the child's headlong dash and to snag him in his arms. "Hi, sport."

"Where've you been?" Joey charged petulantly. "Tuesday I waited and waited, but you never showed up. Aunt Edith's birthday's real soon, and we gotta finish her present."

Kara watched as Bric pushed back the wedge of hair that had flopped over the boy's forehead. "I didn't forget. Something came up. Tell you what. You sand it on Monday. I won't make any promises, but I'll try to fly over Tuesday after school. If you meet me at the airstrip, I'll bring the stain, and we'll see if we can't get the job done."

"At the airstrip? But that's a far way to walk," Joey protested.

"Sorry, pal. It's the best I can do."

"Why can't you come to the schoolhouse?"

"It's been pretty hectic around here lately, Joey. I'm not sure I can take the time."

While he spoke, Bric's eyes were trained on Kara. She nearly reeled from the contempt she saw in their dark depths.

Joey looked from one adult to the other, then fell silent and wriggled out of Bric's arms. Kara realized that with a child's sharp perceptions, Joey sensed something was wrong. She hated for him to be caught in the middle of their personal conflict, but she could do nothing about it.

Lifting her chin a notch, she said, "Hurry up, Joey. We have a plane to catch."

On their way to the aircraft, she could feel two holes burning with laserlike intensity between her shoulder blades.

A half hour later Kara was steering the battered old van toward the schoolhouse. Though her ears picked up the strains of "Row, row, row your boat" from the rear, her mind was back in Sandusky. Over and over she asked why she'd let herself be talked into this field trip. She should have known better than to risk running into Bric.

Just as she was telling herself that she'd simply have to stick to the island, she felt the right wheels veer off the berm. The next instant the van was sinking into a sea of muck.

When Kara finally realized what had happened, she dropped her forehead onto the steering wheel and silently cursed John Brickner. If she'd been paying more attention to the road and less to him, she wouldn't be where she was this minute. *Stuck!*

"All out," she instructed the four expectant faces looking to her for rescue. "We'll have to walk the rest of the way."

A series of groans followed her pronouncement, but the children did as they were told. Feet heavy with mud-caked shoes, they trudged toward the school.

Kara heaved a weary sigh. It seemed as though disasters always came in threes. Since she'd already weathered two in the space of an hour, she wondered what other nasty trick fate had up its sleeve.

She didn't have to wait long to find out. Just as they came slogging up to the schoolhouse, Beverly Oldt broke away from the small group of waiting parents and darted forward. At first Kara thought the woman was suffering an anxiety attack because they were so late getting back, but her first words dispelled that notion.

"Something terrible's happened!" Mrs. Oldt cried when the exhausted little group came closer. "It's Walt Parker. He's had a heart attack."

"When?" Kara asked, drawing Joey protectively to her side.

"Early this afternoon. Lucky for Walt, the noon plane was late, so we were able to get him and Edith on it. That's where they are now. At the hospital in Sandusky. I don't expect Edith'll be back any time soon."

Kara looked down at the small child. His thin face had gone pale. Rubbing his back, she tried to soothe him, "Don't worry, Joey. I'm sure your uncle's going to be fine. Meanwhile, how would you like to stay with Lynn and me?"

"Oh, that's not necessary," Mrs. Oldt interrupted. "We'd be more than happy to take him in." She paused, then shrugged. "For a couple of days, anyway."

Reading hesitancy in Joey's frightened eyes, Kara gave his shoulder a squeeze. "What would you like to do, Joey? Not that I want to take you away from Billy, but Lynn and I would be glad to have you, too. It's been quite a while since I've had a man in the house."

The corners of Joey's lips curved weakly just before he slipped his hand into Kara's.

"This has been the longest week of my life." Edith Parker produced a handkerchief from her coat pocket, dabbed at her eyes and blew her nose. "I don't know what I'm gonna do. It's a lot worse than I thought when we flew Walt to the hospital."

"I'm sorry to hear that." Kara groped for more appropriate words, but they wouldn't come. How could she console the woman when the doctors themselves hadn't been that reassuring? All they'd told Edith was that her husband's condition had stabilized. They weren't certain how long it would take him to recuperate, nor would they make any predictions about when, if ever, he'd return to work.

Mrs. Parker lifted her heavy frame from Kara's sofa. "I can't thank you enough for looking after Joey."

Kara smiled. "He's a delightful child. No bother at all. In fact, it's going to be pretty lonely around here without him."

"The Oldts said they'd look after him, but I'm glad he stayed here. Don't get me wrong. Beverly means well, but she sure keeps that household of hers in a stir. No wonder Billy's such a flibbertigibbet. Comes by it natural, I'd say." Edith frowned. "Joey can do without that kind of commotion."

"I agree."

"I've always worried a lot about that boy. Walt and me...we're so old. More like grandparents. And now with Walt being sick, I don't know how I'm gonna make out when he comes home."

"If I can help, just give me a call."

"You've done enough as it is. A body's gotta go on, that's all. Still, having a child around..." She wagged her head back and forth. "Come on, Joey," she called toward the bedroom where he'd been entertaining Lynn.

"I'm certain everything will work out," Kara remarked, but after she'd closed the door on the older woman and little boy, she admitted to having reservations. Given the situation, she had to sympathize with Edith Parker.

Kara felt even worse about Joey. After his father's death, only a strong sense of family obligation had prevented the Parkers from placing him in a foster home. Now with Walt so ill, it looked as if that might be their only option.

Kara flirted with the idea of having Joey live with her and Lynn, but she dismissed the notion almost as quickly. Even if the social agency approved, she'd be selfish to pursue it. Joey needed a caring father as much as a loving mother, and without a husband, Kara could offer him only half a home. Other children might thrive with a single parent, but Joey needed the security of a traditional family. He'd missed so much in life already.

That fact couldn't have been brought home any more emphatically than it had been the previous Tuesday. Slumping onto the couch, Kara closed her eyes and massaged her temples. She wished she could remember exactly what Bric had told Joey that Saturday evening at the airport, but she'd been so shaken the words hadn't completely registered. All she could recall was that the two of them had arranged to meet after school, but she couldn't say for sure if it had been a firm commitment or simply a possibility.

After making the three-mile trek to and from the airstrip, Joey had been beside himself when Bric hadn't shown up. "When's he going to come back?" he'd pleaded, his chin drooping over the unfinished napkin holder. "He promised he'd teach me how to clean the flue, too."

Knowing the child idolized Bric—more than that, looked up to him as a father figure—Kara had kept her replies evasive. She wasn't willing to admit that the man had no plans to finish what he'd started. With Joey. Or with her.

The rest of the week, her first grader slacked off in his work, often dawdling away class time daydreaming. Soon, Kara knew, she'd have to explain. But she wasn't yet up to facing that unpleasant duty. How could she smooth over the little fellow's hurt and disappointment if she herself broke down?

On the Sunday evening that Joey returned to his aunt's, Kara took an early shower. After slipping into her warmest flannel gown, she tried to bury herself in a current best-seller, but it was a lost cause. With nothing better to do, she decided she might as well go to bed.

March was certainly going out like a lion, she mused as she climbed between cold sheets. At times like these Kara wondered how much longer winter could hold spring back. The dismal weather only intensified her heartache. It was as if nature were holding a mirror up to her soul.

Flipping onto her stomach, she punched up the pillow. She had to forget about Bric. But how could she when no matter where she turned some reminder jogged her memory? Rarely a day passed that she didn't hear the drone of the Cessna as it swept overhead. Always she wondered if he was piloting it, and a fresh anguish would seize her.

Or she would open the cabinet where the Easter baskets she and Bric had so cheerfully filled sat waiting for the holiday, and immediately her throat would close up. How, she despaired, would she ever manage to distribute them without coming apart?

For the next few hours, Kara lay in bed, wide awake. Like a steel trap, her mind clamped on to her quarrel with Bric and refused to let go. She knew she was largely to blame for what had happened. How she wished she could erase her mistakes as easily as she did those on the blackboard!

But with Bric there could be no starting over.

Maybe it was all for the best, anyway. He'd never really loved her, she reminded herself. He'd been drawn to her mainly because of Lynn. What a bitter paradox! Edmund wanted her but not her baby. Bric wanted her baby but not her.

Kara's head throbbed with indignation as she rolled over and picked up her alarm on the nightstand. Rubbing her eyes, she read the luminous dial: 3:00 a.m. When was she ever going to get to sleep? Instead of wearing her out, the mental flagellation that disturbed her days was plaguing her nights, as well. She sniffed in disgust. Why, if she'd never been one to tolerate pity from others, did she continue wallowing in it herself? *And that,* she scoffed, *is exactly what you are doing, Kara Reynolds. Indulging in self-pity.*

As she set the clock back on the table, Kara watched the second hand make another circle of the dial. Another... and then another. Suddenly the lesson of its infinite sweep forward hit her. She couldn't set time back; she couldn't change the past. But she could give herself a good, swift kick in the rear and stop grieving about what was over and done with.

It was time to focus on the future, on everything she had to be thankful for. Kara slid under the covers and counted her blessings. She had Lynn. She had her job. And she had her health—for now. If she wasn't careful, she would wear herself down, and she couldn't let that happen. Too many children depended on her. She needed to get outside, breathe fresh air, walk until she was ready to drop.

Yawning broadly, Kara promised herself that tomorrow, if it wasn't raining, she would take the children on an island field trip.

On that thought, sleep finally came.

"It's not April Fools', is it?" Joey asked when on the following morning Kara announced the outing. Already Ruth and Ralph had tricked him into believing he'd ripped his jeans, and he wasn't about to be taken in again.

"No, it's not April Fools'. Now, get your boots on," she instructed him kindly. "It's still a little wet outside."

Kara had already made arrangements to drop her daughter off at Mrs. McCann's and save the older woman a trip to the school. While the children argued over who got to push the stroller first, she heaped wood in the stove, hoping a roaring fire would chase out the damp air in the classroom.

"Okay, everybody. Be sure you have pads and pencils. We're going back to that safe area of the woods we checked last fall. Now that warmer weather is just around the corner, there should be lots of changes."

As Delia and Sam led the eager parade out the door, Kara caught her sixth grader by the coat sleeve. "Just a moment, Billy. Aren't you forgetting something?"

"Aw, Mrs. Reynolds, do we gotta take notes?"

For answer, Kara pointed him toward his desk.

Over in Sandusky, Pam was giving her brother an equally hard time. Ever since she'd found out about the rift between Bric and Kara, she'd been after him to go patch things up.

"You know you're in love with the woman," Pam accused him, standing in the middle of his kitchen. "And, what's more, she's in love with you. So what's the problem?"

"The problem is, she put one over on me," he answered, irked at having to argue with his sister for the second time in an hour.

"Because she didn't tell you her former husband was alive? Big deal!"

"Maybe it wouldn't have mattered so much if I hadn't been up front with her. But I was. Besides, what really rubs me the wrong way is that she never told Reynolds about his own child." A muscle in his jaw tensed. "I've learned my lesson. Never trust a woman. Any woman."

"Tsk, tsk. Such a sexist philosophy. I could take offense, but under the circumstances I'll let it pass."

"Generous of you," he grumbled, resigned to letting his sister have her say. He was getting damned tired of trying to sidestep her arguments. He snatched a kitchen chair and straddled it backward.

"Watch your mouth," Pam chided him. "On second thought, I like you better when you're spoiling for a fight."

She plopped onto a chair near him and laid her hand on his arm. "I'm sure Kara had good reasons for holding back. With you and with... What's her ex-husband's name?"

"Edmund."

"Thank you. Edmund. Maybe he didn't give her a chance to tell him about Lynn. About anything. Did you? Or did you hop on your high horse and ride off into the sunset?"

"When a woman plays me for a fool, I'd rather not know her reasons."

"Aren't you overreacting?" Her tone twisted the question into a reproach. "Which only goes to prove my point. You love her, Johnny, more than you've ever loved any woman. Otherwise you wouldn't feel this wretched over what I'm sure is an oversight that can easily—"

"Oversights. Plural."

"Don't be so nitpicky. Kara's very warm-hearted and loving. I liked her right off."

"Now look who's jumping to conclusions. You're around the woman all of two hours, and suddenly you're a character witness."

Pam shrugged. "Experience ought to count for something. Even if I weren't older and wiser—which I am—I'm a quick study."

Bric knew what she was up to, but he refused to be pacified. "How come you were blessed with such astute genes? If that's a family trait, it sure as hell missed me." He drew in a breath. "It's over, Pam. And nothing you can say is going to change that."

"Okay, little brother, it's your life."

"And I'd appreciate it if you'd let me live it the way I want."

"Humph!" Pam got up in an exaggerated huff and went for her coat. "You call what you're doing living?"

After she had left, Bric sought the seclusion of his library, where he always did his best thinking. Absently he picked up a volume of Alexander Pope and flipped through the leather-bound book. He noticed a passage he'd underlined years earlier: "A man should never be ashamed to say he has been wrong, which is but saying in other words that he is wiser today than he was yesterday."

Cursing, he slammed the book shut. Bric considered that he'd made his share of mistakes and had always owned up to them. But had he come away the wiser?

He laughed mirthlessly. This time he sure as hell had. Kara had seen to that. Clever teacher that she was, she'd hammered home the lesson that integrity wasn't to be found in the female of the species. Unfortunately, that bit of wisdom didn't make it easier to forget she lived only a few minutes away.

Nor could Bric forget it later that morning as he sat at his office desk.

Absently, he snapped a pencil in half and threw the jagged pieces among the rest of the clutter. Why couldn't he get Kara off his mind? He stared at the charts in front of him, swearing. He'd let it happen again, allowed a woman to sandbag him. He hadn't expected Kara to fight dirty. But she'd packed a hell of a punch.

He knew he couldn't go on this way. For days now he'd survived on anger alone, working nonstop in an effort to shut Kara out of his thoughts.

Sometimes he hadn't even bothered to go home but had spent the night on a couch in his office. And even when he had, he'd scrupulously avoided his bed. The truth was, he'd only gone into his room to change clothes. Whenever he'd walked through the door, he could swear he smelled Kara's light floral scent.

Bric spun around and stalked to the window. He stared out at the bright April day, which was so at odds with his mood. Shouldn't he be immune to despair by now? Able to tough it out? What was it he'd heard once? Something about pain making a man stronger in all the broken places. Only it didn't work that way. Not for him. Not when it came to Kara.

He whirled away from the window and strode back to his desk. He picked up the broken pencil and rammed the splintered halves together. At this rate he was going to drive himself crazy. Why did he keep wondering how Kara was, how Lynn was, how Joey was, even how Delia and Sam were getting along? He hadn't fallen in love with only one woman but with a baby, a whole school, an entire community.

Bric rubbed the back of a hand across his forehead, suddenly reminded that he still had to help Joey finish his aunt's gift. So far he'd been unable to face flying to Perry's and had assigned Steve Johnson the run.

Not that the switch had done him much good. No matter how hard he tried, he couldn't eject Kara from his thoughts. Her face was everywhere. Especially vivid were her eyes swimming with tears when he'd accused her of lying.

The more he replayed that quarrel, the more his conscience nagged him. Maybe he hadn't been fair. He'd been so consumed with his own hurt and anger, he'd hardly heard what she'd said that morning. Even now he was unable to recall the details of their argument.

Could Pam be right? Was he making a mountain out of a molehill? Granted, Kara had covered up the fact she was divorced. But at the same time he hadn't given her a chance to tell him why her marriage had gone sour.

Then, too, there was Reynolds. Come to think of it, something about the man bothered him. Why hadn't he shown more enthusiasm about being a father? As far as that went, why hadn't he been ticked off with Kara for keeping his daughter's birth a secret?

All at once there were too many questions and too few answers. Bric didn't like leaving things between him and Kara dangling. No wonder she haunted his every waking moment.

The passage from Pope he'd read a few days earlier stole into his mind. But this time he saw it in a different light. He hadn't acted wisely at all. He'd judged Kara guilty without ever hearing her out.

Bric grabbed for his jacket. He owed it to Kara, to himself, to listen to what she had to say. But what if she didn't want anything to do with him? His features hardened as if carved in stone. He wouldn't leave until he had the whole story.

Frankly, Bric didn't give a damn what it was, either. The important thing was that he loved Kara. If only she could forgive him for being a pigheaded jerk!

He yanked the receiver off the hook and dialed the hangar. "Brickner here. Tell Steve to wait for me. I'm flying to Perry's on the noon plane."

"Looks like somethin's burning pretty good down there," Steve noted laconically as the Cessna made its approach for landing. "That the schoolhouse?"

From the passenger seat, Bric had paid scant attention to the familiar terrain below. Kelleys Island,
South Bass, Middle Bass, North Bass, the lake. He
knew them all as well as the back of his hand. For the
most part he'd given Steve's small talk barely polite
responses. He was preoccupied with Kara. How would
she react when she saw him? It wasn't quite noon yet,
so most of the children should be around. In particu-
lar he was counting on Joey to help ease the strain.

At last, Steve's observation filtered through Bric's
detachment. He shot forward in his seat and squinted
through the windscreen. "My God, it is! Get this bird
down, Steve. Fast!"

At the schoolhouse, fiery tongues licked at the roof
and snaked over the back windows. Black smoke rose
in ugly plumes to darken the April sky. People were
shouting and running around, bringing every available container to the volunteers who were already on
the scene, pumping well water and forming a bucket
brigade. Vaguely Bric wondered where they all had
come from. Every able hand pitched in to help.
Someone shouted that the winery sprayers were on
their way, their tanks filled with water. In the absence
of a fire department, the sprayers served the island as
hose trucks.

Drawn into the midst of this orderly confusion, Bric
fought panic as he searched for Kara. He coughed as
a down draft brought a whiff of acrid air into his
lungs. Though his skin felt seared by the heat of the
raging fire, his blood ran as cold as ice water.

Where was Kara? In desperation he grabbed hold of an older man who was passing buckets along the line. "Where're Mrs. Reynolds and the children?"

"Don't rightly know, but it appears nobody's in the schoolhouse. I expect they're out and around somewheres."

Relief flooded over Bric. Beside himself with worry, he'd been ready to dart into the flaming building on a one-man rescue mission if Kara or any of the youngsters were trapped inside. He noticed that the fire seemed confined to the back, that unless overcome by smoke, everyone had surely been able to get out the front entrance. All the same, he wanted to see for himself, know for sure that they were all right.

Lynn! He turned back to the man. "What about the baby?"

"Mrs. McCann's got her. Over there." He nodded toward a small group, his hands busy with the buckets of water.

Torn between wanting to help and needing to assure himself that Kara was safe, Bric threaded his way to the edge of the crowd, where the older woman stood watching.

"What about Kara? The children?" he bellowed over a sudden clamor at the arrival of the sprayers.

"Don't worry, Mr. Brickner." During a break in the din, she elaborated, "They're out in the woods. Haven't gotten back yet for lunch."

"How did it start?"

"Can't tell you. Here come Delia and Sam. Maybe they know something."

Bric rushed toward the young couple. "What happened?"

"Beats me," Sam croaked, disbelief starkly etched on his face. "Must have been that old stove. Mrs. Reynolds stoked it up real good this morning."

Bric let loose with a vicious expletive. He should have seen to that flue. He would have, too, if he hadn't been so bullheaded. "Where is everybody?"

"They oughta be back soon. They weren't far behind us. We left a little early to catch the plane for high school."

With the help of the sprayers, workers quickly got the flames under control. Most of the roof was gone, and it appeared that the back of the school sustained the worst of the damage. Fortunately the fire had been checked short of Kara's apartment.

Just then Bric caught sight of Joey running toward the still smoldering schoolhouse, Kara on his heels. Bric's long strides brought him to the boy first. In a quick lunge, he gripped the six-year-old around the waist and lifted him, kicking and screaming, off his feet.

When Joey saw whose arms were wrapped around him, he stopped his wild flailing. "I want to get my present. What if it burned up?"

Bric set the child on his feet and capped his shoulders, anchoring him in place. "It's probably fine. If it isn't, we'll make another one."

"Really?" Joey clapped his hands, then had an afterthought. "But we worked so hard on this one."

"And you learned a lot, didn't you? Enough to do it again. We can always make another napkin holder, Joey. But we can't make another you. Don't ever try to run into a burning building to save things. No possession's worth risking your life for."

"Okay. But I bet you'd have run in to get us out if we were in there."

For answer, Bric tousled the boy's unruly thatch of hair. Turning, he caught sight of Kara's stricken face. Her eyes were wide with shock. Without a word, he walked over and folded his arms around her shaking body, gathering her close.

"I'm sorry," he murmured into her hair. "I'm so sorry. But all that matters is that you and Lynn and the children are safe."

"Oh, Bric, if I hadn't taken the class out today..." She squeezed her eyes closed in an effort to blot out the horror her imagination had conjured up. "If I hadn't left Lynn at Mrs. McCann's..."

"Hush," he rasped. "Don't think about it." Gently he rocked her to and fro in his arms.

"Does this mean we don't have school tomorrow?" Joey questioned, yanking on Kara's coat.

Both Kara and Bric had to laugh. They stooped and sandwiched the boy between them.

"Probably not, but don't wish for a long vacation," Kara cautioned. "Otherwise, you'll have to make up the time in June."

"Shoot!" Joey pulled free of the adult arms. "Then I hope they get it fixed tomorrow."

Kara gave him an understanding smile. "I imagine we'll find another place to hold school in the meantime."

The boy's face brightened as a new idea presented itself. "If we don't have school tomorrow, maybe Mr. Brickner and I could work on my napkin holder." He looked up expectantly.

"I'm afraid I'll be tied up, Joey. The way I've been these past couple weeks. But we'll get back to it soon enough. Scout's honor. I'll call you about when. Okay?"

Kara watched as Joey rapidly swapped disappointment for happiness. *How resilient children are,* she reflected. Leaning down, she cupped his face in her hands. "Meanwhile, Joey, I need your help. I don't want anyone running into the building to get anything. It isn't safe. Would you pass the word around?"

Once Joey had left, Bric regarded Kara with admiration. "Nicely done. He won't try to get inside if he thinks he's in charge of keeping everyone else out."

Before she could respond, the school board president broke into their exchange. "Thought you'd like to hear, Mrs. Reynolds, we're having an emergency meetin' tonight to get this thing straightened out. Probably have a good old-fashioned school raisin'. About time we got modern heating in that building, anyway."

"Thanks, Mr. Mullins. I appreciate it."

"Meanwhile, if you and the baby got nowhere to stay, me and the missus'd be proud to put you up—"

"That's kind of you," Bric cut in, "but Mrs. Reynolds is staying with me."

Mr. Mullins missed the astonished expression Kara threw Bric, and tipped his hat. "Well, then, we'll report back to you after the meetin' tonight. Got a phone number where I can reach you?"

Kara blocked Bric's hand as he drew out a business card for the board president. Though still dazed by the fire and his unexpected appearance, she wasn't about to be conned into spending the night at the man's house. It wasn't so much a matter of should she, but could she. Things were far from resolved between the two of them.

Kara touched Mullins's coat sleeve. "Why don't I phone you when I'm settled. I'm not sure how long I'll be at Mr. Brickner's."

"Whatever you say. For now we'll board up the school. Don't want nobody gettin' hurt."

When they were alone, Bric put a finger beneath Kara's chin and lifted her face to his. "We have some talking to do. That's why I'm here. The fire... God, Kara, when I saw the blaze from the air, I was never so terrified in my life. I thought I might have lost you." He touched her cheek. "You're not getting away again. I'm taking you and Lynn home."

"Bric, I don't think that's a good idea."

"How can you be sure until we talk?" he asked with indisputable logic. "No arguments."

Too shaken and weary to put up a fight, Kara didn't object when he tucked her against his side and led her toward Lynn.

Chapter Thirteen

Kara cracked open the kitchen door and allowed her eyes the pleasure of roaming over Bric's length. As he folded back the sleeves of his khaki shirt and bent to check the water level in the coffeepot, she felt a familiar tug at her heart. Retreating a step, she told herself that she mustn't give in to her emotions, not when doubts were swirling through her mind.

What, she brooded, had prompted Bric's insistence that she take refuge with him? He'd said they needed to talk, that he'd come looking for her before he'd ever known about the fire. But how could she be sure he wasn't merely being charitable? It wouldn't be the first time she'd been an object of John Brickner's benevolence.

Equally distressing was another suspicion. One she'd kicked around for many days and nights. Was she nothing more to Bric than a convenient means to instant fatherhood? After all, he'd never once told her he loved her. Not even when he'd asked her to marry him. At the time she hadn't given the omission a second thought. Only later had his words come back to mock her. She remembered distinctly how his proposal had been coupled with the idea of making them a family, how he could then be a "father to Lynn."

And yet Kara couldn't discount Bric's actions that afternoon on Perry's. Hadn't his eyes held more than a kindly solicitude when he'd found her amid the confusion in the school yard? Hadn't his frantic embrace telegraphed something besides simple compassion? Was it possible that he did care for her, not solely because of Lynn, but for herself alone?

On that tiny glimmer of hope, Kara took a fortifying breath and pushed open the door.

As she stepped into the kitchen, Bric glanced over his shoulder. "Sunshine okay?"

"Sound asleep. For once she didn't finish her bottle."

"How about you?" He pivoted to face her. "Over the worst of the shock?"

"I think so. At least my knees have stopped shaking."

"That's a start." Bric motioned toward the stove. "I'm fixing us some lunch. You hungry?"

"Maybe a little." Their conversation was so guarded that Kara had to dig her nails into her palms to keep from wringing her hands. Decidedly unnerved, she asked, "What can I do to help?"

"Would you mind setting the table? I thought we'd have grilled cheese, tomato soup and coffee. Sound all right?"

"Sure." Acutely aware of Bric's nearness, Kara quickly located plates and bowls and laid them by the stove.

"Almost ready," Bric finally announced. "Have a seat."

Kara did so, wondering how he could look so sexy, standing there with a soup ladle in one hand and a pot holder in the other. As he flipped the sandwiches from an iron skillet onto their plates, she nearly yielded to a crazy desire to rush over and wrap her arms around him.

"Dig in," Bric commanded, placing a steaming bowl of soup and a golden brown sandwich in front of her. "You're probably hungrier than you think."

Kara tried to use the food as a barrier against awkwardness, but she succeeded in doing little more than pushing the spoon around her soup bowl. When at last she braved a close look at Bric, she thought she detected a deepening in the fine lines radiating from his eyes. Could he possibly have lost as much sleep over their quarrel as she had?

But the hope that again swelled Kara's heart was quickly dashed. What difference would it make? She would never be able to breach the gulf of distrust that lay between them—a gulf that was all the wider for Bric's conviction that she'd betrayed not only him but Edmund. Abandoning all pretense of an appetite, Kara removed her spoon from the bowl and laid it on her plate.

Bric lingered over his coffee, his hooded eyes never leaving Kara. Until she'd taken off her coat, he hadn't noticed how much weight she'd lost. He wanted to take her in his arms and kiss away all the hurt of the past weeks. But if he acted on that urge, they'd never get around to talking, and they owed it to each other to clear the air.

Surveying Kara's barely touched lunch, Bric observed, "You aren't doing justice to my culinary talents. Grilled cheese is my specialty."

"Don't be offended." She fingered her unfinished sandwich. "It's no reflection on your cooking."

"That's a relief! Seriously, though, can't you force down a few more bites?"

"Please, no lectures." Were the five pounds she'd lost over their breakup that obvious?

"Very well." Bric slid away from the table and tipped back his seat. "Since you're the teacher, I'll leave the speeches to you."

Kara attempted a smile. "My problem is I can't think of a good opening line."

"How about, 'I've missed you'?"

"Is that what you think? That I've been pining away?"

The front legs of his chair smacked the floor. "Well, haven't you? I sure as hell missed you."

Kara quirked an eyebrow.

"You find that hard to believe?"

"In a word, yes," she returned, perversely discounting his haggard appearance. "Aren't you the one who refused to speak to me? Or do I have the wrong man?"

"I walked right into that, didn't I?" Bric rubbed a hand across his chin. "But can't you see? That business about your husband threw me. I thought I knew you. I never dreamed you'd—"

"I wanted to explain," she broke in. "You didn't give me a chance."

"Guilty as charged." Bric gave her a sheepish grin. "I can be pretty hotheaded at times. I apologize." When she failed to respond, he remarked, "That was your cue to say, 'Apology accepted.'"

He looked so contrite that despite herself, Kara smiled. "Apology accepted."

"Now that we've got that settled, it's your turn. Honest, Kara, I want to understand. Tell me what happened between you and Reynolds. Why did you...," He faltered, unsure how to ask without appearing to accuse.

"Lie?" she supplied. "I told you it wasn't deliberate. As for Edmund, that's another story."

"I'd like to hear it."

Kara probed the compelling depths of his eyes. Was it conceivable that she could get through to him, make him see things from her perspective? Maybe. But even if she did, she still wasn't convinced it would change anything. Nevertheless, she knew she had to try.

Half in anticipation, half in dread, Kara asked, "Where should I start?"

"Why not the beginning?"

"Okay." With slow deliberation, she rested her wrists on the table and folded her hands. "When I first met Edmund, I was barely eighteen. Wherever he went, he turned female heads. I admit I was as dazzled as the next woman, but it wasn't his looks alone that attracted me. Edmund had a disarming charm that was impossible to resist. Anyhow, I was flattered when he asked me out. It was a plus that both of us seemed to enjoy the same things—art, opera, literature."

Kara paused, reflecting. "I could scarcely believe my good luck when he proposed. But we hadn't been married long before he started staying late at the office. At the time I thought a noble heart beat under all that ambition.

"But I couldn't have been more wrong. It took me a while, but I finally figured out that Edmund wanted only one thing from life—success. So when he found a higher ladder to climb, he grabbed it." At Bric's puzzled look, she clarified, "Another woman."

"He was a fool to let you go."

"Hardly. The truth is, his desertion was carefully calculated. Monica wasn't just any woman. Her father was a justice on the state supreme court. Not only that, the two of us had grown up together." Kara stared at her clasped fingers. "I thought Edmund's mistress was his work. I never dreamed she was my best friend."

Bric reached out and covered her hands with his. "My God" was the only comment his husky voice could get out.

Struggling to compose herself, Kara took a sip of coffee. "The crowning blow was that he told me about Monica the very day I learned I was pregnant."

The revelation seemed to siphon all the air from Bric's lungs. He threaded his fingers through hers. "So that's why you didn't tell Reynolds about Lynn. You had too much self-respect to tie him down that way."

"I was also too angry. My telling you I'd lost my husband was no Freudian slip. I'm ashamed to say I started wishing Edmund was dead." Tears trembled on her lashes. "What's worse, I used Lynn for revenge. In some twisted way, I imagined I could punish him by keeping her to myself.

"Not until he walked out did I look at my marriage objectively. I came to realize Edmund wasn't the man I thought I'd married. Yet you taught me that in spite of the grief he'd caused me, in spite of his weak character, he was still entitled to know about his daughter." Kara looked up, wiping at her moist eyes with the back of a hand. "Isn't it uncanny how things sometimes turn out? I'd already planned to take Lynn to meet him. Only he showed up on Perry's first."

Bric gently rubbed his thumb over her knuckles. "Will he be wanting visitation right?"

"He's not the least bit interested in Lynn."

With a resigned sadness edging her tone, Kara related all that had passed between her and Edmund during his brief visit. When she'd finished, Bric commiserated, "You've had a hell of a lot to contend with, haven't you? I'm so sorry. You deserved better."

Tilting her chin at a proud angle, she protested, "Don't shed any tears on my account. I'm much stronger for all that's happened."

"No need to convince me. I've always admired your courage. What do you think captivated me in the first place?"

"Lynn," she blurted out.

"Lynn!" Bric's expression was one of complete disbelief. "Where did you get such a ridiculous idea? I admit I love Sunshine as if she were my own, but that has nothing to do with how I feel about you."

Kara regarded him with steady eyes, carefully weighing his words. Finally, she ventured, "How *do* you feel about me, Bric?"

"What kind of question is that? I asked you to marry me, didn't I?"

"But you never said you loved me."

Bric's jaw went slack. He spent a long minute searching his mind before he asked, "I didn't?" When she shook her head, he wavered. "Are you sure?"

"Positive."

"No matter," he quibbled defensively. "My actions spoke for me."

"Your actions spoke of desire. That's not the same as love."

"It is where you're concerned."

"A woman likes to hear the words."

"A mere technicality," he persisted, his eyes touching hers. "But if it's that important..." Bric drew her onto his lap. Gathering her close, he whispered in a voice rough with feeling, "I love you, Kara."

A spiral of joy rocketed through her. Leaning back, she gazed into his eyes. "Tell me again. I want to watch while you say it."

"I love you. And I love Lynn. I wish I really were her father. I envy your ex-husband that."

With the utmost tenderness, Kara's fingertips traced the rugged line of his jaw. "My darling, don't you know there's a world of difference between fathering a child and being a father? You're already more of a daddy to Lynn than Edmund will ever be."

Profoundly moved, Bric buried his face in her hair. "You say the nicest things."

"While we're on the subject of *our* daughter—" the emphasis rolled easily off Kara's tongue "—there's something else I've been meaning to tell you. It has to do with her middle name."

"Joan? What about it?"

"Did you know it's the feminine counterpart of John?"

"It is. My name? Hey, I like that!"

"Good. Because I named her for you."

"You did?" Overwhelmed, Bric searched for an adequate response. "I don't know what to say. I feel so honored."

"I'm glad you're pleased."

"It's the best gift I've received. But I don't understand. Why me?"

"My flights of fancy," she replied directly. "I couldn't shake this image of what it would be like if you, not Edmund, were Lynn's father. I think you swept me off my feet the moment you walked into my classroom. And with each passing day I fell deeper and deeper in love." The smile on her lips wobbled. "That's why I couldn't work up the nerve to tell you about Edmund. I was afraid of alienating you. The more of my heart you claimed, the more I had to lose."

"Kara, I can't tell you how happy you make me." Bric tightened his hold on her. "I love you so. It's going to take me a lifetime to show you how much."

"Then hadn't you better get started?" she suggested coyly.

Bric lifted a strand of hair and let it float through his fingers. "I like the way you think, lady. But first we have an important decision to make."

"About what?" Kara laid her temple against his cheek. She didn't want to talk. She only wanted to feel. Rough against smooth, hard against soft...man against woman.

"Our wedding date," Bric murmured between tickling nips on her ear.

"How am I supposed to think when you do that?" The question came out on a soft rush of air. "Let's decide later."

"That's a deal. But you have to agree not to make me wait long."

"Whatever you say." Her lips skimmed over his, sampling their flavor.

"What an easy woman!" Bric teased before his mouth smothered hers in a kiss that set off explosive fires throughout Kara's body, scorching every nerve ending. She felt his hands go to work on the tiny pearl buttons of her blouse. Within seconds his agile fingers had bared her to the waist. Whimpers of feminine delight mingled with groans of masculine pleasure as first his callused palms, then his tongue glided over her exposed skin.

Intoxicated by wave after wave of sensation, Kara was only remotely aware of sliding from Bric's lap. When her feet touched the floor, he whispered something at her mouth, but she was far too engulfed by need to comprehend the words.

As if caught in a gently swirling eddy, they made their way toward the hall. Lips still fused, they swayed up the staircase, articles of clothing strewn in their wake. At the top of the steps, Bric swung her into his arms and sidled through the door of his room.

With exquisite care he lowered her crossways on the bed. Quickly he rid them of their few remaining garments. Folding his hands around her face, he brought their mouths together. Warm lips teased. Impatient hands tormented. Soon their breath was coming in rapid, shallow pants.

Bric was reminded of the first time they'd made love. He'd wanted to take it slow, to prolong the enjoyment. For himself. For her. But that had been as impossible then as it was now. He couldn't hold himself back. Not with Kara's slender fingers straying downward to close intimately around him. The air stalled in his throat as he grated, "Kara, Kara, I..."

It thrilled her to bring him so much pleasure. When her caresses evoked a series of tremors, she smiled in delight.

Suddenly Bric grasped her hands. "Enough, darling. You're killing me." Easing her onto her back, he kissed her with such skill that in no time she was feverish with passion, begging him to end the sweet agony.

She arched and took Bric into her, gasping at the force of his desire. Faster and faster, deeper and deeper, he drove her to the final peak of pleasure and the explosive beyond. Even when her world splintered into millions of tiny fragments, each with its own shimmering color, he didn't stop, but carried her higher yet for a second, even more shattering spasm of rapture. Over and over she chanted his name, her voice merging with his repeated cries of "Kara." Through the hazy fog of her mind, she was barely conscious of Bric collapsing on top of her, scarcely aware that the earth seemed to have fallen right out from beneath them.

Kara didn't know how long she slept nestled in Bric's arms. When she reluctantly opened her eyes, she measured the rays of the sun streaming through the curtained windows. By the length of the shadows she guessed that it must be early evening. Now that April was here, the days were growing longer. She smiled. With Bric at her side, no day would ever be long enough.

She dropped a light kiss at his throat and was rewarded with a low growl. He stirred slightly, his breathing steady and deep. Blindly he reached out and closed his hand over one breast.

Almost light-headed with euphoria, Kara lay very still. She felt blissfully happy, totally at peace. What a day it had been! When she'd climbed out of bed that morning, she had no idea that she would be sleeping in Bric's arms by evening. Or that Lynn would once again be tucked into the beautiful cradle in the next room.

Kara hadn't heard a peep out of her baby in hours. Deciding she really ought to check on her, she carefully disengaged herself from Bric's embrace. As she swung to her feet, her eyes caught the precarious tilt of the bed. Muffling a giggle, she hurried out to the hall and gave in to a fit of laughter. *Better get a grip on yourself,* she admonished herself, *before you wake the household.*

By the time Kara opened the door to Lynn's room, she'd managed to conquer her mirth. Cautiously she tiptoed toward the cradle and peered down at her still sleeping daughter. Her eyes softened as she ran a finger over one baby-soft cheek.

The loving gesture called up a vision of Joey. He was always lavishing Lynn with attention, talking to her, showing her his drawings. He'd make a terrific big brother, Kara thought, realizing how terribly she'd miss him if he had to find a new home. And it looked more and more as though the Parkers would be unable to keep him. How hard it would be for them all if he had to leave.

Suddenly it occurred to her. Why *should* Joey be thrust into unfamiliar surroundings? Why should he have to be separated from his family and friends? Now that she and Bric would be marrying, he could make his home with them. Kara decided then and there to talk to Bric. She was certain he would be as excited about the prospect as she was.

Warmed by her plans, Kara slipped back into Bric's room. At the sight of the sloping bed, her laughter again erupted.

"What's so funny?" he grumbled, pulling her down beside him.

"Wake up, sleepyhead, and see for yourself."

Braced on an elbow, Bric was startled to find the bottom of the mattress tipped at a twenty-five-degree angle. "What the hell!" he muttered as he shifted to the edge and peered under the bed at the mattress support.

Slowly he brought his gaze back to Kara, a satisfied grin splitting his face.

"How many?" she asked.

"Three. Out of five."

"Mmm, three out of five. Not bad."

"What d'ya mean, not bad?" he mimicked.

Kara couldn't contain her merriment.

"Now what's so funny?"

"I was just thinking. Most earthquakes register anywhere from one to nine on the Richter scale. Maybe," she suggested, "we need our own measure. We could call it the Brickner scale and base it on the number of slats we shake loose when we make love. What do you think?"

"I think you should be quiet." Bric slid a possessive hand behind her.

"Why?" Her mouth twitched with amusement.

"So we can try for four."

"Four? We're stopping at four?"

"Who said anything about stopping?" With a broad smile, Bric hauled her into his arms.

* * * * *

1989
IS THE YEAR
OF THE MAN!

What makes a romance? A special man, of course, and Silhouette Desire celebrates that fact with *twelve* of them! From Mr. January to Mr. December, every month spotlights the Silhouette Desire hero—our **MAN OF THE MONTH.**

Sexy, macho, charming, irritating…irresistible! Nothing can stop these men from sweeping you away. Created by some of your favorite authors, each man is custom-made for pleasure—*reading* pleasure—so don't miss a single one.

Diana Palmer kicks off the new year, and you can look forward to magnificent men from **Joan Hohl, Jennifer Greene** and many, many more. So get out there and find your man!

Silhouette Desire's

MAN OF THE MONTH…

MAND-1

Silhouette Special Edition

MORE SPECIAL THAN EVER,
SAY THESE TOP AUTHORS:

JO ANN ALGERMISSEN

"To me, writing—or reading—a Silhouette Special Edition *is* special. Longer, deeper, more emotionally involving than many romances, 'Specials' allow me to climb inside the hearts of my characters. I personally struggle with each of their problems, sympathize with the heroine, and almost fall in love with the hero myself! What I truly enjoy is knowing that the commitment between the hero and heroine will be as lasting as my own marriage—forever. That's special."

TRACY SINCLAIR

"I hope everyone enjoys reading Silhouette Special Editions as much as I enjoy writing them. The world of romance is a magic place where dreams come true. I love to travel to glamorous locales with my characters and share in the excitement that fills their lives. These people become real to me. I laugh and cry with them; I rejoice in their ultimate happiness. I am also reluctant to see the adventure end because I am having such a good time. That's what makes these books so special to me—and, I hope, to you."

SSE-A2

Silhouette Special Edition

COMING NEXT MONTH

#505 SUMMER'S PROMISE—Bay Matthews
Burdened with grief, Joanna felt empty, old, weary of living. But when her estranged husband, Chase, appeared on her doorstep, need and desire took hold...and a new life began.

#506 GRADY'S LADY—Bevlyn Marshall
Ladies' man Ryan Grady had tangled with Blythe Peyton's type before—blond, beautiful, deadly. He had to protect his brother from her poison, no matter how sweet it tasted....

#507 THE RECKONING—Joleen Daniels
Once, Cal Sinclair had offered her an ultimatum. Laura Wright had chosen college over marriage...and Cal had chosen Laura's sister. Could heated passion ever sear away burning regrets?

#508 CAST A TALL SHADOW—Diana Whitney
Juvenile investigator Kristin Price was gutsy, but a harrowing stint on Nathan Brodie's ranch for delinquents truly tested her courage. Even for love's sake, could she confront her most intimate terrors?

#509 NO RIGHT OR WRONG—Katherine Granger
Single mother Anne Emerson didn't need another man—or another scandal—messing up her life, and her best friend's ex-husband was a candidate for both. Somehow, though, being wrong had never felt so right.

#510 ASK NOT OF ME, LOVE—Phyllis Halldorson
Was Caleb's past too dangerous to speak of—even to his love? What terrible secret had made him dodge Nancy's questions and desert her in a time of need?

AVAILABLE THIS MONTH: